SPACE

by

MARTIN HUGHES

CHIMERA

Space Captive first published in 1999 by
Chimera Publishing Ltd
PO Box 152
Waterlooville
Hants
PO8 9FS

Printed and bound in Great Britain by
Caledonian International Book Manufacturing Ltd
Glasgow

SPACE CAPTIVE

Martin Hughes

Chapter One

Real fear gripped Liz. Her hands were moist as they clenched the control handles of the auxiliary quasar cannon behind the bridge. Blinking sweat from her eyes, she tried to sight on one of the fast moving pirate vessels converging on her crippled cruiser like hyenas to a stricken antelope back on Earth.

The whole ship lurched sickeningly, putting her off her aim, as it took another crippling hit. The acrid smell of burning plastic and insulation was sharp. Flaring her delicate nostrils she tried to find more cool refreshing air. Hot under her combat armour, she shifted uncomfortably as a bead of sweat trickled down the curve of her spine and between her buttocks. She braced her legs farther apart to keep her balance on the tilting floor, knowing it was really just a matter of time because the ship could not take much more of this punishment.

Although not particularly fearing death, capture by these pirates – tales of their depraved barbarity preceding them – had always been at the back of her mind when on operations in this sector. Now it was uncomfortably in the forefront of her mind! She tried sighting on another of the swarm, to take her mind off things as much as anything else, but her concentration lapsed as she considered how she had arrived in such a predicament.

She recalled her pride on passing out of the Euro space academy of Brussels, back on Earth. Hers were the top marks of her class in astro-navigation, and the highest ever marks for a British girl. There were many who thought that with a face like an actress, lustrous long dark hair, and a curvaceous body to match, she would be better gracing the 3D tele-vid screens rather than a space uniform.

However, Liz was determined to live life to the full in space for a few years and then, just on her twenty-third birthday when she had indeed thought about settling down, she had been made second-in-command of the Solar Federation's newest space cruiser, *Explorer*. It was an unprecedented achievement for one so young to achieve such a position, and a dream come true – especially under the command of its present captain. She had fallen in love with Harry when he had been her tutor at the academy and, although their relationship had never – then – been consummated, she knew he loved her too. Now their feelings were their own secret, never to cross into their professional lives. Although they were lovers when on leave, in space it was purely business and Liz won the respect of most of the hundred or so officers and junior ranks below her.

This was *Explorer's* second long cruise in the virtually lawless Magellan region of space, and it had been proving just as successful as the first one in stamping out the activities of the pirates. The pirates felt, due to their vast distance from Earth, that they were above the universal laws of mankind which, it had always been agreed, should apply equally to all who colonised space after the miesonpower drive was discovered in 2030. This finally allowed ships to exceed the speed of light. Only vessels such as *Explorer* could try to bring a measure of lawfulness to the outer regions and prevent such illegal activities as the hijacking of raw materials and selling on the black market, and hostage-taking.

Explorer, though, had been more successful than most previous ships. At four hundred metres in length and ten thousand tonnes in weight, and with its superior armaments, it could devastate any known opposition.

Both Liz and Harry had heard rumours of 'wanted' signs with their pictures on them springing up on the outer worlds, but had felt safe enough within the mighty walls and defensive shields of their ship. They had not, however, counted on the sabotage during their last overhaul which had disabled some of her vital systems while still over two weeks' distance from the nearest help. Nor had they foreseen the armada of small pirate ships that had been waiting for them in a prearranged ambush while they were answering a distress call from a non-existent cruise liner.

Liz was suddenly jerked back to the present when a blast of air nearby sent her crashing to her knees, protected only by the thick insulation of her body armour and helmet. She thought it must be the end, and then visions of Harry drifted into her mind. She desperately wanted to be with him one last time, and began to ease herself to her feet to get to the bridge where he had been trying to fly the crippled ship.

But suddenly the metallic floor started vibrating around her, announcing someone's arrival.

Liz looked up expecting to see some of her battle-weary crew, but was shocked to find herself staring down the barrel of a needle-beam gun. A gruff male voice addressed her from the impersonal spacesuit towering over her.

'Surrender or die! It's over!'

Liz instinctively tried to lunge at him, but all too late she sensed the movement of someone else behind her. The crack of a stun gun was the last thing she heard before darkness enveloped her.

When Liz's senses returned she found herself lying uncomfortably on a floor, still in her space armour but devoid of any weapons. Loops of wire bound her hands behind her. Her head ached abominably from the effect of the stun gun – but she knew from experience that that would soon pass.

She spotted several of her crew lying in a similar predicament, and from the bouncing movement of the floor she guessed they were in a small pirate shuttlecraft. Everyone was anonymous in their suits, unless close enough to read their name flash on the shoulder. To her dismay though, glancing round from her limited viewpoint, she could not see Harry's distinctive captain's echelons.

Her stomach churned; surely they hadn't killed him? A captain was a good bargaining chip with the Federation. It might be that her own second-in-command insignia had spared her when she had tried to fight back at her capture. Then she realised that in its place was a jagged hole in her outer suit, probably from the blast of a phaser.

A terrible bleak emptiness engulfed her. Perhaps he had died fighting – as maybe she ought to have done. The uncertainty of his fate gnawed at her, yet she daren't compromise him, or her, by asking.

Eventually the shuttle docked with another craft and Liz began her new life in captivity. As she and her crew were herded down corridors to a holding area she saw other prisoners, and it gave her hope that Harry might have been on another shuttle. Although their hands were unbound they all had to lie face down on the floor. Their external suit microphones were switched off and sacks were pulled over their helmets to leave them in mute, helpless darkness.

She heard several gruff commands from their captors, and received a painful kick in the side until she lay in exactly the position required. She knew it would be useless to demand humane treatment for her and her crew. Their only hope was total compliance until they could assess the situation. Apart from the surnames on their suits, their captors would have no idea as to the identity or sex of their prisoners. But as Liz lay obediently immobile, she knew it would only be a matter of time before identities were discovered.

At last rough hands aggressively hauled her upright and hustled her along, pushing her in the back and pulling her by the arm. After a while the sack was pulled off her head, and she was in a smallish room with a man and woman. Their demeanour was slovenly and they wore clothing that marked them as pirates.

A pile of discarded spacesuits and clothing took up one wall.

The armed guards who had manhandled her to this chamber stood back, but Liz was more wary of the cruel-featured pair who now addressed her.

'Get the suit off,' snapped the woman. 'Get everything off. We'll check you before you're taken to planet-fall. Your precious Federation may have planted bugs or sensors on you in a futile effort to get you back. Now hurry – get it all off.'

After removing her gauntlets and unscrewing the helmet, Liz heard snide laughter as the pirates saw her properly.

'Well, well – it seems we've hit the jackpot,' the man leered, licking his thin lips like a lizard. 'It would appear we have in our midst the infamous Liz Hartley, second-in-command of our enemy's most powerful ship. I remember her from the posters and the news-vids. Get it all off, girl. I've seen articles about you – interviews too; the Fed's pin-up.' He laughed again. 'And I have to say, you're as horny in the flesh as you are on the screen... Now hurry, or I'll have to do it for you.'

Despite trying to steel herself, a red flush of shame covered Liz's delicate cheekbones as she reluctantly took off the bulky suit and finally stand before her captors in her blue one-piece coverall. Suddenly, without the protection of her ship and its awesome technology, the glamorous life of a space crusader had taken a new turn. It was one thing to seek out and destroy pirate ships while punching computer buttons, but this new reality, face to face with the hated enemy, was entirely different.

She felt terribly, vulnerably afraid. Despite that, she gathered her courage and tried to face up to the responsibilities of command. 'Look, I don't know who you are,' she said, as forcefully as she could manage. 'My name is Elizabeth Hartley. I am second officer of the Federation cruiser *Explorer*, and I demand to know how many of my crew are prisoners and what has happened to my captain—!'

Liz's brave speech was brought to an abrupt end as one of the guards suddenly doubled her up with a vicious jab to the ribs. The pirate in charge looked amused, and waited for a few seconds while the beautiful girl held her side and struggled to fill her gasping lungs.

'Prisoners may not talk,' he said calmly. 'You lost all rights when you set out to destroy us free traders. Not so brave now though without your fancy ship, are you?

11

We don't care who you *were*, girl. You're just a prisoner now – our prisoner. You're not a second-in-command any longer, so the number and identity of our prisoners is not your concern. All you have to do from hereon in is obey orders – our orders. If you talk again you'll regret it. You'll be questioned later, but right now...' he licked his thin lips again, 'you will take your clothes off.'

Although only a humble pirate lieutenant, Tarik was also relatively intelligent and knew how humiliating this would be for the beautiful female gingerly holding her side and grimacing with the pain of the guard's punch. In a short space of time she had been defeated in a skirmishing battle, stripped of her power, security, and status, forbidden even to talk, and was now having to undress before the very enemies she had been trained to despise and hunt and kill. He felt a stirring in his loins as, looking down to avoid his eyes, her hands lowered the zipper of her coverall and she peeled it of to reveal her superb body covered only by a skimpy white bra and panties.

Her hands crossed over her thrusting breasts as she looked up again at her tormentors, hoping her undressing would be sufficient.

Tarik knew that her flimsy feminine covering was too small to significantly conceal anything, but he saw no reason to deprive himself of a rare treat. He'd seen the odd news footage of the glamorous Federation commander being interviewed. Now he wouldn't have to rely upon his fertile imagination. Besides, he had his orders.

'Get it all off. Or do you require assistance?' He watched a stray lock of her lustrous dark hair flick across her face as she shook her head. Then watched eagerly as she reached behind to unclasp the straining bra, enjoying the way she submissively kept her eyes downcast as it dropped to the floor, before slipping her fingers into the waistband of her dainty panties, bending gracefully, and easing them down her slender legs with a delicious rustle.

'Undo your hair, let it down,' he ordered, when she was quite naked before his appraising eyes.

Fighting to contain her seething anger, Liz obediently reached up to unpin the several clips still holding her hair in place. She shook her head and her long tresses cascaded in a dark waterfall over her creamy smooth shoulders.

Tarik again licked his lips in appreciation. Suddenly the previously impersonal figure, so dangerously capable, was transformed into a vision of lush and vulnerable femininity.

'Give me your watch; you'll not be needing it any more,' he continued relentlessly.

She unstrapped the expensive diamond timepiece Harry had given her so recently, and handed it to her tormentor. It meant so much to her, and yet he merely glanced at it indifferently and stuffed it into his pocket.

'Hands on head, legs astride, open your mouth wide,'

Tarik ordered. A muscle twitched in the corner of his eye as he lecherously assessed the vision before him. She was somewhere in her twenties, he guessed. She was no longer a renowned officer of a predatory space cruiser, but simply a naked woman, and an exquisitely beautiful one at that. Her mouth-watering breasts were tipped with button-hard nipples, and the hands on head posture offered them so temptingly to him. Her flat and neatly muscled tummy led to shapely hips, and then to slender thighs and legs. Making her stand with her mouth open, displaying perfect white teeth, was ostensibly to see at a glance if a prisoner had concealed anything there before the search proper. It also added to the victim's feelings of humiliation and total subservience.

The captive stared defiantly ahead as her tormentor slowly walked around her, the heels and toes of his boots clacking on the metallic floor. All the while the cruel-looking woman with him sneered as she watched the spectacle with obvious relish and smoked an evil-smelling cigar.

Tarik stopped. Liz held her breath and expected the worst as she felt his vile gaze crawling over her back and tensed bottom, and then he moved again to kick away the delicate undergarments which had, until so recently, snuggled warmly against her feminine intimacies. A silent sob formed within her as she recalled Harry buying her those delicious wisps of lace; never dreaming they would ever be viewed in such

14

terrible circumstances.

Liz remembered how she and Harry had been due an off-duty day and had planned to spend it together. Tears formed in her large brown eyes as she realised just how dramatically events had changed since they made those plans. Harry might not even be alive, and she was now a helpless captive of the pirate empire.

She jumped from her brief reverie, startled as she felt the man's hand pat her bottom with sickening and unwelcome familiarity.

Tarik smiled as the soft yet toned globes flinched under his touch. He ventured further, and lightly stroked the silken flesh of her delightfully smooth buttocks. Never before had he felt and eyed such beauty. He stepped a little closer, breathed deeply her fresh fragrance through flared nostrils, and allowed the slight swelling in his trousers to brush fleetingly against her bottom, transmitting a clear message to her. He enjoyed her faint shudder of revulsion, and then slowly, so as to prolong her humiliation and his pleasure, he moved his hands up over her hips, her ribcage, and then finally cupped and weighed her firm yet silky soft breasts. The nipples stiffening instinctively beneath the balls of his thumbs, and made his groin lurch further with anticipation.

'You had a lover onboard your ship, I think,' he said casually into her ear. 'A very lucky man, I'd say.'

'No, I—'

'No? Then why else would you wear such... such

15

provocative undergarments?' he goaded smugly, and then before Liz could answer he patted her superb buttocks one last time, dragged himself away from her, and turned to his female accomplice. 'Check her over,' he licked his lips again and grinned, before adding, 'thoroughly…'

Tarik knew full well his captive had absolutely nothing concealed on her body, but while he processed the paperwork on her he enjoyed the arousing sight of his companion spitefully pulling her this way and that, prodding and probing with nasty relish. And he also enjoyed the occasional whimper of protest from the determined yet helpless beauty at their mercy.

His companion, the sadistic Dork, was nearly twenty years older than her victim and had lost a husband at the hands of the hated Federation. Thus she particularly enjoyed dealing with such prisoners. Tarik glanced up from his notes just as she pushed Liz roughly against the bulkhead, making her lean against it on outstretched arms and then kicking her feet wide apart and ordering her to stand on tiptoe. With the cigar planted firmly between clenched teeth, its fumes combining with Liz's trepidation to make her feel nauseous in the pit of her stomach, Dork felt beneath her prisoner's lustrous hair at the nape of her neck and shoulders. She felt under her warm armpits, and then down her sides. Liz shuddered at the icy touch. Dork continued down and over the pert cheeks of the hated captive's bottom. Smiling evilly over her shoulder at Tarik, she pushed a

16

finger between the firm globes and watched them clench instinctively around it. She paused. Her victim was holding her breath. She glanced at Tarik again and saw she had his complete attention, the paperwork forgotten. She looked back at the captive and leaned close. 'You scum!' she hissed in her ear, and then without warning she stabbed her straightened finger past the valiant sphincter muscle and into Liz's secret passage.

Liz gasped and arched her back as the vile digit violated her. She closed her eyes and called upon her inner-strength to help her through the ordeal. It came as no surprise when she felt more intrusive fingers crawl around to the soft dark down between her thighs and seek out her ripe sex lips. A thumb began rubbing in circular motions until her clitoris responded, while the fingers delved into her wet warmth. She squirmed and dropped onto the soles of her feet. Dork snarled, lips curling against the soft hair at her pounding temple, ordering her to strain up again onto tiptoe. Liz couldn't stop herself from panting softly, and her breasts rose as she filled her lungs with the stagnant air. Her traitorous hips gyrated slightly, and then Dork suddenly pulled away and Liz sighed.

'She's clean,' Dork smirked crudely, 'but the little whore was getting to like it!'

Tarik watched Liz's proud head sink between her straining shoulders as she struggled bravely to maintain her uncomfortable position against the bulkhead. Her toned legs quivered enticingly. Without urgency, he continued with the paperwork as Dork bawled at her captive for trying to ease down from her aching toes.

When he had finished he moved to the gorgeously despondent figure. He swept his broad palm down and violently slapped one fleshy buttock, and his cock lurched again as she gasped and flinched helplessly and a pink blotch spread out on her smooth skin.

'We're done with you here,' he said curtly. 'Put on the clothing we've provided and you'll be taken to a reception centre at our headquarters. And let me remind you once again – no talking is allowed whatsoever.'

As he spoke Liz thankfully relaxed from the uncomfortable position and took a bundle of coarse clothing from Dork. It consisted of a pair of baggy trousers with a drawstring at the waist, and a loose top which was held together by just a couple of buttons; most of their companions were missing. It was yellow with thin white stripes, ridiculously ill fitting, and there was no underwear.

Having struggled into the garments Liz had to roll the long sleeves up a couple of times, and then bent agilely from the waist to do the same to the oversized trousers. Both Tarik and Dork looked on hungrily as the material stretched tightly over her buttocks like a second skin. When she straightened again Dork roughly pulled Liz's hands behind her back and fastened her wrists with plastic cuffs. She then hung a badge with a number fifteen printed on it around the persecuted girl's neck. Finally she retrieved from the pile on the floor

18

Liz's expensive underwear, and crudely drew them slowly across her face.

'I'll keep these, I think,' she slavered, her eyes watching Liz closely for any reactions. 'You'll not be needing them where you're going.'

Tarik leaned close to Liz, and she could smell his sweat. 'I'll be watching your progress, number fifteen,' he said, in such a manner that Liz did not doubt him. 'We'll meet again, I can promise you that.' He stared blatantly down at the deliciously tempting shape of her breasts hiding beneath the baggy striped top. 'And when we do… well…' he chuckled in a way that made Liz shiver with dread, 'let's just say I'll have me some fun. You might not enjoy yourself, but that doesn't really matter too much, now does it?' He chuckled again, and then one of the guards stepped forward and Tarik handed him a folder, nodded once, and the guards led her out and along a gloomy corridor.

The shuttle-flight to the planet was extremely uncomfortable. Liz and several other members of the crew, all wearing identical attire and numbered with badges around their necks, were strapped into seats with their wrists still fastened behind their backs. They sat in groups of four. Still forbidden to speak, they could only smile at each other with a silent reassurance that clearly none of them really felt.

Despite the gravity of the predicament, Liz realised that the crewmember sitting opposite her, an inexperienced teenager named Kirk, was having great difficulty in tearing his eyes from the front of her shirt, where the gaping material allowed him to feast unhindered upon the beckoning shadows of her deep cleavage. She closed her eyes and groaned inwardly; any authority she still held over her crew, and which would be needed for when they attempted an escape, would be quickly eroded by such familiarity. It was clearly a deliberate psychological ploy on the part of the pirates. What lengths might they go to in their attempts to completely nullify what little power of command she still retained? Liz had known for some time that for many of her male crewmembers – and possibly even some of her female crewmembers – she was a fantasy figure, but in the structured and disciplined world of the Federation she could never be anything other than that. Now, however, the well-respected guidelines had been shattered, and Liz was all too well aware that to certain members of her crew she was now vulnerable and accessible.

She opened her eyes, and the tented material in the teenager's lap confirmed her worst fears. She blushed under such undiluted adoration, and had to admonish herself for having difficulty in dragging her gaze away. She glanced quickly up at Kirk's face, concerned he might have caught her looking at his obvious state of arousal, but his unblinking eyes were still avidly glued to her cleavage. Her eyes were drawn inexplicably down again, and an electric thrill caused her nipples to stiffen as she saw the tent twitch quite clearly. She preyed Kirk could not see the evidence of her inexplicable feelings poking against the baggy cotton shirt. The roughness of the material compounded the agitation to her nipples as she breathed. She hated herself for such emotional weakness, but couldn't deny that the sight of the aroused teenager and the knowledge that it was her body that was having such a devastating effect upon him was making her quite hot and flustered. Her mouth felt dry, and she was inexorably swamped by a craving to close her lips around the hidden but undoubtedly engorged tip. To suck the evidence of his homage into her mouth, and feel it stretch her lips and nudge the back of her throat as, judging by the impressive dimensions of the bulge, it clearly could…

Liz shook her head and clenched her fists to get a grip on herself, and at that moment the shuttle bumped gently as it touched down, and her intensive survival training and instincts immediately returned to the fore.

The doors hissed open, pirates boarded, unfastened their prized cargo, and unceremoniously led them out.

To Liz's horror there were reporters with vid-cameras to witness the shame of the crew of the Federation's most powerful and feared ship being led away into captivity. Liz guessed they were from neutral colonies who would transmit around the civilised worlds for all to witness the humiliating downfall; heroes and heroines of the Federation being herded around as miserable prisoners of war by a rag-tag band, their awesome cruiser defeated by tiny outdated pirate vessels. It would make excellent propaganda for the pirates, thought Liz gloomily, as she and the others had to shuffle slowly past the cameras in their belittling outfits, showing their captivity numbers, wrists bound behind their backs. She wondered how her many friends back on Earth would react to the sight of her, dishevelled and defeated... nothing more than a statistic of the guerrilla war.

Suddenly her spirits soared as she caught sight of Harry. He was alive! The man she loved was alive! Maybe she could now endure the coming ordeal – whatever it may bring – after all.

Harry, too, felt elated when he saw Liz. His heart went out to her, barefoot in her baggy outfit. He saw she was number fifteen. He was number sixty-nine, their allocation obviously random, just part of the de-humanising process. Harry accepted that they were just puppets now in the hands of these bastards, and knew their duty was to endure whatever atrocities were thrown at them without supplying any information that might compromise the Federation's security.

He gave silent praise to the designers and builders of *Explorer*, for counting mentally, it seemed the vast majority of the crew had survived the battle. He glanced anxiously across at Liz on the other side of the sparse cold room, careful not to give the watching enemy any indication that he and she were an item. That would make things far too dangerous for both of them.

A huge barrel-chested and heavily moustachioed

pirate stepped before the demoralised rabble.

'Right, listen up!' he bellowed. 'It's shower time for you filthy imperialist scum! Numbers one to forty will shake your arses and get over here in a line! Now! Numbers forty-one to ninety will go when they return! Now move it, you slags! When I give an order you jump! You are not imperialist soldiers any more – you are scum prisoners!' He emphasised his point by viciously slashing his baton down through the air. 'I want you all lined up tit to arse, tight together, no gaps as you lead off into the shower room. And the same when you're going through the shower. Keep it snappy and keep together. You'll get to know each other real well, I reckon,' he guffawed.

With a feeling of utter helplessness Harry saw his beloved Liz squashed into the tight line with sergeant McDuff, one of their largest and most repugnant crewmembers, pressed snugly against her softness from behind. Harry could imagine the rating's lower regions eagerly thrust against Liz's buttocks as they shuffled off to the showers. Their enforced silence allowed them to hear clearly into the shower room and Harry grit his teeth again when he heard the shouts and orders from within.

'Get their cuffs off. Right, all of you, strip. I want you all buck naked except for your numbers – keep them on. I want a tight line, tit to arse, tit to arse. I don't want to see no light between you. Press together, go through in a chain, slowly, keep pressing together.'

Approximately a third of the crew were women, but such sensibilities didn't mean a thing to this rabble. Liz found it shamefully embarrassing to be naked amongst her crew, but there was simply nothing she could do. The jets of warm soapy water hissed, a roaring tattoo beating onto their bodies. She found herself having to push her slippery body tight against lieutenant Rose Pierce in front of her.

Rose had been newly promoted to head of personnel on *Explorer*. The firm cheeks of her rounded bottom were tight against Liz's pubic bush, and her own soft breasts were squashed against the delectable curving spine of the girl. Liz had to get a grip of herself; she was responsible for all of these people, and the acute danger they shared.

Liz had no difficulty in turning her mind to matters other than the soapy body pressed against her erect nipples; she was sickened by the huge presence of sergeant McDuff behind her. Liz had never liked the man and his ways, and he never really seemed to accept her as his senior officer. Now he took full licence as she felt his thickening manhood pushing hard up between the globes of her soapy bottom, and the coarse hair on his chest scouring her back. His large hands brushed her hips unnecessarily as they shuffled through the showers.

After the line had slowly moved through they had to repeat the process, but with plain water to rinse them. A third time through and hot air blasted out to dry them.

At the end each crewmember had to stand with hands above their head, slowly turning while delousing powder was puffed onto them.

Liz looked away as a grinning pirate made Rose turn her inviting body oh so slowly while he applied the powder, even taking the liberty of rubbing it into her feminine curves. Then he slapped her bottom to send her scampering off to find her discarded outfit.

Next it was Liz's turn, and the same humiliating performance before the grinning gap-toothed man. As she turned like a ballerina, Liz couldn't help but notice the smirk on McDuff's face, drinking in her beauty; a beauty the slob had probably drooled over in his dreams or while she gave him orders he resented. She had to look away as he took full advantage of the situation and pointedly ogled her thrusting breasts, and then down at his own semi-stiff organ swinging between his solid thighs, lifting slightly to point in her direction.

There was no way to escape the familiar hands of the pirate, smoothing the horrible smelling powder onto her groin and belly and breasts, and patting her bottom to indicate she could move on and dress.

Like pale ghosts under the thin coating of powder the prisoners, hand-cuffed again, were led back to the main hall. Liz caught Harry's eye before he and the others in the second batch were taken for their showers.

When they were brought back they sat in silence on a bench opposite Liz's group. The pirates had caught two crewmembers whispering to each other, and the excessive lashing the man and woman received from a crop ensured that no one else infringed upon that order.

Time passed slowly. Liz guessed it must have been evening by the ship's time. She was tired and hungry, but then a stir went through her crew as the barrel-chested pirate stood before them again.

'Interrogation time, ladies and gentlemen,' he said grimly. 'You will each be questioned individually and your stories then cross-referenced. I think you already understand that it would be extremely unwise to lie. Now, numbers one to six will stand to be taken for questioning.'

Harry tensed as four men and two women from his crew were led away. More time passed slowly, more numbers were called out, and more of his crew disappeared.

And none were brought back.

Harry knew the time would come, but it still hit him like a mule kicking his stomach, when Liz's number fifteen was called out. Their eyes met briefly. Then a dusky-skinned pirate, who was guiding her by the arm, obscured Harry's view as he led away his beautiful Liz, second-in-command of the mighty *Explorer*, to an unknown fate.

Chapter Two

The dwarfs were bred to carry out engineering work in deep space within the confined access of the engine rooms of space cruisers. When the cost of putting a payload into space could be measured in terms of a year's salary per kilogram of weight it made good economic sense to make use of genetic engineering to create such dwarfs. With the good pay available to them the dwarfs were happy, and they ensured that the mighty space engines kept turning. However, with the newer miesonpower driven ships, the dwarfs were often no longer required. Originally bred for a purpose which now seldom existed, they were naturally bitter and often penniless, tending to drift towards the dregs of planetary low-life. The natural in-breeding, which occurred after society lost interest in its little space engineers, also created more and more unbalanced and deformed dwarfs.

The shrunken, embittered creatures always sent an unconscious shudder through Liz, and she'd always avoided them whenever possible.

And so she cringed when, after leading her silently along endless corridors, the bronzed pirate ushered her into a gloomy tiled room occupied by such a hideous-looking dwarf. The squat, barrel-shaped troll-form rose, the close-set eyes under a bulbous forehead glinting in the half-light. The characteristically long fingers, at the end of powerful muscled arms, flexed in anticipation.

Liz shivered, trying to take a step back as he shuffled forward, but the pirate's iron grip only allowed her to shrink back a little.

'Oh, what a pretty one,' the dwarf slobbered, a thin blob of spittle escaping his thick lips as he clambered up onto a nearby chair to match her height. Liz jumped, pushing back against the pirate's body as the dwarf's bony fingers reached out and cupped her chin, turning her contorted face this way and that. The piggy eyes then glanced down at the gaping front of her tunic, and she whimpered as a finger jabbed the softness of her breasts.

'Nice,' the dwarf said appreciatively.

'Enough, Mungo.'

Liz could have cried with relief as a severe-looking woman in a white medical coat and thick pebble glasses appeared and admonished the dwarf with a withering stare. He slipped off the chair and shambled away a little, muttering sulkily.

'Release the prisoner's hands,' commanded the woman, and Liz thankfully rubbed her aching wrists as the pirate removed the cuffs that had confined her for so long.

'Leave us,' the woman ordered the dark pirate, moving to stand before Liz as the man left and the door hissed shut behind him.

'You've met Mungo, I see,' the woman continued to Liz, her cold magnified eyes crawling up and down the baggy outfit. 'I hope you will not give him cause to get angry; he can get quite carried away when he's angry. He's especially protective towards me.' She smiled, ruffling the thin hair of the squat creature.

'In case you weren't aware of it,' the woman continued, turning her attention back to Liz, 'you and your ship have caused us much trouble, here on Magellan, so it's very good to actually have you with us – here in the flesh, as it were. Talking of which,' the woman pointed dismissively, 'take off those ridiculous pyjamas.'

Liz wavered, her hands automatically clasping the neck of the top together, looking anxiously at the squat figure by the woman's side.

'Please, not in front of…' Liz whispered. 'May I—'

Her hopeless protest was halted by the surprisingly strong and rapier-like hand of the woman. Two teeth-rattling slaps left and right made her stagger back in shock, clasping her stinging cheeks and shaking her head to clear her buzzing ears. She couldn't recall the last time she'd been slapped like that.

'You insolent slut,' spat the woman. 'You dare to question my orders? You had better forget your previous notions of who you are, your authority, what you should and shouldn't do, and in front of whom – and you'd better forget them quickly. You are a prisoner of this breakaway nation, and this nation consists of various oppressed peoples under the thumb of the Federation. However, the Federation isn't here to help you now, and you are no longer in your fancy ship of destruction. You are here, and you are about to be questioned. Those to be questioned are always required to be naked; it helps to concentrate the mind. If the body is laid bāre then the mind too will follow. You will now obey my previous order and strip of your own accord, or Mungo will do it for you. Rest assured, you would do well not to try my patience.'

Liz looked apprehensively at her tormentor, but found no warmth in the staring eyes behind the thick antiquated glasses. Surely, as a woman of authority herself, thought Liz, she would know what she was asking of her – to undress under such circumstances. However, the uncompromising woman just stared, waiting, and so, hesitatingly, Liz unbuttoned the shirt. There was silence in the chamber, apart from a low electrical buzz and the rustle of discarded clothing as Liz reluctantly let the baggy covering drop at her feet in a puddle of pale yellow.

The woman and the dwarf savoured the sight of Liz's naked charms, one arm crossed over her rapidly rising and falling breasts and one hand covering her soft pubic down. Liz remained immobile, barely daring to breathe, as the loathsome pair walked behind her.

She felt tempted to move a hand to cover her bare bottom, but that would only have drawn attention to it. All she wanted was to be anywhere but in this chamber under such scrutiny. If only the floor would open up and swallow her.

'Oh!' Liz yelped and jumped as a calloused hand stroked one cheek of her bottom. She shuddered, feeling sick at the touch.

'She's so smooth, madam,' wheezed the dwarf. 'She's like silk.'

'I've told you not to touch until I give you permission,' admonished the woman, accentuating her warning with a brisk cuff to the dwarf's head. 'Now, let's get started. We have a lot to process today. Secure her, Mungo.'

Liz tried to isolate her mind from her body as the dwarf manhandled her into the position he required. She had initially pulled back, but she knew the strength the dwarfs possessed – and this Mungo was no exception. Although he was half her size and she was no weakling, she was like a baby in his hands.

The diminutive creature twisted and cuffed her wrists painfully behind her up between her shoulder blades, so she had to stoop forward a little to ease the strain on her arms.

'Oooh, lovely,' the dwarf giggled, as Liz's posture thrust forward her shapely breasts. His long fingers briefly squeezed her soft swinging orbs, then lightly patted them, giggling again as they wobbled in his hands.

'Oh, stop it, please,' begged Liz, but the dwarf just grinned, easily side-stepping a kick she aimed at him before carrying on his task of binding her.

An arm, with sickening familiarity, encircled Liz's waist and guided her to a large metallic grill, raised from the floor and resting horizontally between two supports. Lightly slapping her bottom he made her get up on it, kneeling, and strapped her ankles wide apart.

The woman looked on. The ritual of binding always amused, but in this case it excited her too. The sight of the delicious morsel at the mercy of Mungo, who undoubtedly disgusted her as his hands slithered, tightening straps and surreptitiously probing, was hugely erotic. And it was also a necessary part of the breaking-down process to make the subsequent questioning that much easier.

Liz was naked and helpless, now unable to move anything but her head. Her bound wrists had been fastened to a ceiling pulley and raised so she had to kneel erect on the grill, painfully bent forward so that her torso was virtually parallel to it. Her bare breasts were nicely vulnerable. The little fiend patted the curved tightness of her buttocks, thrust out immodestly by her posture, her ankles being fastened about half a metre apart. She shuddered in helpless disgust, shivering as his fingers traced over her tautly curving nates. Being forced to kneel with her weight on her knees against the slats of the grill caused considerable discomfort. Her bent posture also caused fiery arrows of pain to dart along the protesting muscles of her back, which she longed to straighten.

The long fingers then moved to her nipples, pinching and squeezing, making Liz gasp in pain, until they became shamefully erect in his hairy hands. She looked in wide-eyed horror as he fixed a clip-on remote control electrode to each of her traitorous buds. They looked like ornate body jewellery, and each one had a glinting micro-chip concealed under a tiny green glass bulb. Liz looked down, aghast, wincing at the pain from the tiny serrated jaws biting into her sensitive flesh.

Finally, the dwarf made Liz open her mouth by pinching the soft flesh of her inner thigh in a cruel pincer-like grip. Then, as her mouth opened instinctively to register a protest a ball gag was thrust between her lips and strapped in place. The rubbery taste and smell of it stretching and filling nearly made her choke. But she'd thought they wanted to ask questions, and she had her set answers ready to reel off – just like in training. So why had they gagged her?

The woman, sitting at a desk just before Liz, noted the surprise in her eyes. 'You are wondering why the gag,' she said. 'Well, firstly my dear, I give a demonstration of what you can expect if you lie, or fail to tell the whole truth. And frankly, I don't want to be deafened by your screams. Then, when I feel you are actually ready to answer correctly, Mungo removes the gag and off we go.'

At the mention of his name, the dwarf pulled up a small seat next to the desk so that he gazed up into Liz's imploring eyes a metre or so from his own curious piggy ones. The woman handed him a tiny control panel and Liz flinched back, trying to guess the effect on her when the dwarf touched one of the buttons on it. The woman spoke into a recorder.

'This is Stern, of Area Seven of the Magellan Free Trading Empire questioning Elizabeth Hartley, former second-in-command of the enemy vessel *Explorer*. This interview is timed as commencing at ten-seventeen Magellan time, the twenty-second of September, twenty-two thousand and two.'

She then turned off the machine.

'Now, I'm sure you planned to say all sorts of dull things about demanding your rights and about how you should be treated and so on and so on, and then providing just the information they train you to back on Earth.' She smiled at the look of uncertainty her words had on her captive. 'Yes, we know all about that. But I want to get all such nonsense out of the way from the start. Then you can just concentrate on answering the questions I ask, totally truthfully. Remember, we shall be cross-checking with your crew, and I'm sure they will be more than sensible with their answers. So, first of all, let's get the unpleasantness out of the way, shall we?'

Stern nodded to the dwarf.

Horrified, Liz saw, as if in slow motion, one of his fingers crawl across the panel and depress a button.

'Arghh...!' Liz squealed through the gag as her right nipple erupted. The awful pain lanced deep into her being. She tried futilely to jerk away, but in the process only succeeded in wrenching on her shoulders, causing even more suffering. She could really only shake her head, eyes screwed tight shut, toes curled until finally the agony subsided.

Her eyes opened again and she blinked away the salty sweat that stung them. With dread she looked at the calm bespectacled face of her tormentor.

'We mustn't leave the other side out, now must we, my dear?'

'Pluh—!' Liz tried to plead through the gag, but she saw the horrible finger move to another button and this time her left nipple erupted into burning agony.

The torture continued for several more minutes. The calmly persistent voice haunted Liz and the cadaverous face swam before her eyes, asking her over and over if she was quite sure that she was ready to answer truthfully.

Was it worthwhile them removing the gag for the questioning proper to begin?

Another bout of suffering shook Liz as Stern's head again nodded to the grinning dwarf. When the mists cleared before her eyes, she cringed to feel a warm wetness between her thighs and hear a dripping sound and the dwarf giggling. She had released her bladder, splashing onto the grill.

Stern looked down, shaking her head and tutting scornfully.

Liz could only sob behind her gag in her shame and

35

humiliation as the dwarf joined in by clapping like an imbecile at what he had made her do.

By the time the gag was blessedly pulled from her aching jaws, all thoughts of evasion and her scant training for such situations had been driven from her mind. The Federation had no right to expect her to endure such horrendous treatment, thus she had no compunction about telling her interrogator just what she wanted to know – within reason, of course.

Before Stern switched on the recorder again she reminded Liz about the ease with which she could be disciplined if she was not co-operative enough. The ugly creature, who could make her world explode into agony with one flick of a finger, nodded and grinned alongside her.

And so the interrogation began.

'You are Elizabeth Hartley, the former second-in-command of the terrorist cruiser *Explorer*?'

'I... y-yes, I am from the Federation cruiser *Explorer*,' Liz stammered.

Stern switched off the recorder and nodded to the dwarf.

Liz opened her mouth to protest but he jabbed a button and red-hot pincers of pain shafted into her breasts before she could do so.

Stern remained expressionless as Liz's pitiful screams echoed around the austerely tiled chamber. When the panting captive had regained her senses the calm voice was addressing her again.

'You will refer to it as a terrorist ship because, here, you are a terrorist. You will also address me as ma'am. I will no longer refer to your rank, because your rank means nothing here. Is that quite clear, or do we need to give you another little lesson on how to behave correctly?'

'N-no... I... I understand.' Liz shook her head emphatically, but another, albeit smaller tweak of fire lanced across her sore nipples, making her writhe in her bonds again.

'I repeat, ma'am is the correct form of address, Hartley, and I want you looking me in the eye at all times. Do you understand?'

'Yes... sorry, ma'am,' panted Liz, ensuring she looked only at the woman who controlled her – controlled her pain.

'Right, then we'll go over that first question again,' Stern said, resetting the machine.

'You are Elizabeth Hartley, the former second-in-command of the terrorist cruiser *Explorer*?' Stern repeated.

'Yes, ma'am,' whispered Liz, shamefully, the words hurting more than the physical torture ever could.

'And you are answering questions of your own free will and not under duress?' Stern gave Liz a meaningful look.

'Yes, ma'am.'

Stern felt a lovely warm feeling between her thighs, rubbing them together surreptitiously beneath the cover of the desk, as she made the beautiful girl before her crawl verbally, conscious of the frightened eyes looking constantly into her own. She was certainly a beauty, she thought, glancing at the proud breasts jutting down, looking even prettier adorned with their crowning green caps of pain. The subdued lighting of the chamber was just sufficient to see the soft sheen of perspiration coating her captive's supple body. She could certainly have any man she wanted simply by clicking her fingers. Stern, however, had always found her own road in that direction decidedly more rocky. Unmarried, the wrong side of fifty, she found that her main pleasure now was in questioning helpless prisoners. And the *Explorer's* capture had certainly netted her enough raw material to play with for some time.

'How many vessels of this empire has your ship destroyed?' she continued.

'I think... I think twelve, ma'am,' answered Liz, fearful of the revenge her answer might provoke.

'And do you know how many of our people were killed during such aggressive displays of destruction?'

'N-no, ma'am.'

'Do you care?'

'Yes, we – we've only ever wanted to stop the illegal trading. We've never wanted to—'

'Stop snivelling!' Stern snapped contemptuously. 'I'll help you, shall I?' She continued without awaiting a response. 'You have recently murdered well over six hundred men and women from this empire, Hartley.

Do you regret that?'

'Yes… ma'am.' Her response was only just audible. 'Of course I do.'

Indeed, Liz did regret it. At that precise moment she regretted it more than anything. No more gung-ho heroism. She was faced with the painful realities of capture, torture and incarceration by the enemy, and she regretted anything which prolonged that pain. The whole interrogation had not gone as she'd been led to expect by the so-called intelligence department back home. She'd not been asked for any technical details of her mission. She was slowly being led across to the pirate's viewpoint – or it would sound that way to anyone listening to the taped version of the interview.

Finally though, with the politics and propaganda out of the way, Liz was questioned at length about the ship and the mission, and she was able to give the partially guarded answers they had all been trained to give. A little voice inside her warned that maybe she ought to have told the truth more fully, especially if other crewmembers did, but she wasn't going to betray all the secrets of her ship.

Then a totally unexpected question was casually tossed in towards the end of the session.

'Who was your lover on board ship, Hartley?'

'I… um, n-no one, ma'am,' she managed, cringing at how unconvincing she sounded. 'I had no lover on board.'

'Interview with Hartley terminated at eleven-fifteen

39

hours.'

The woman turned off the machine and addressed her prisoner.

'Your eyes tell me you are lying, Hartley, and I don't like being lied to. I've no time now to find out who your lover was, but I will. I'm sure someone will tell me, and then we'll talk again.' Stern nodded to the dwarf.

Although she guessed he was going to release her, Liz still flinched back slightly, as far as her confinement would allow, as the nasty troll approached her, wiping a dribble of spittle from his slack mouth on the back of his hand. She tensed as his fingers unclipped the awful electrodes from her sore nipples and the blood painfully throbbed back into the sensitive flesh. She moaned as the beast briskly rubbed the circulation back into each pinched bud, closing her eyes in helpless disgust as the hands mauled her precious breasts.

At last he released her ankles and wrists. She groaned in relief as she, at last, had the luxury of supporting herself on all fours, her head hanging down and her face partially obscured by a dark curtain of lush cascading hair. She winced with pain as the dwarf grabbed her arm and helped her down from the grill. She would have eased herself down gingerly, but he simply jerked her stiff limbs. He then looked on appreciatively as, without thinking, she pushed her hands into the small of her back, arching it to relieve the ache, but at the same time inadvertently thrusting her bare breasts forward. His eyes drank in the supple bow of her body from her shoulders, covered in a mantle of black hair from her thrown back head, to the firm hollowed cheeks of her tensed bottom.

'Lovely...' he drooled, as Liz realised the display she was offering the pair and hastily covered her nudity with her hands and arms as best she could.

'Now, the pretty bird has to go in the cage,' he said, hauling a rope on another pulley. Liz looked as a large cage swung down and the dwarf secured it at waist-height, and then unlocked and opened its door.

'I can't...' began Liz, looking in disbelief at the tiny space she was expected to squeeze into. But his insistent grip on her arm brooked no refusal.

'In, girl,' he prompted, pointing at the metal cell with his free hand.

Liz could hardly believe that she could fit into such a small space, but she did manage to clamber in, feeling the dwarf's disgusting groping hands on her bottom as she did so. She was confined in a stooped crouch on the balls of her feet, her breasts squashed against the tops of her thighs and her head and neck bent down awkwardly. The bars of the cage were too close together for her arms or legs to protrude through, so she could gain no relief or extra space by squeezing her limbs between them. Such a cramped confinement was another torture in itself, and she knew she would soon ache intolerably.

Suddenly she felt herself being lifted, swaying into

the air as the dwarf yanked a rope and tugged her cage behind him along an overhead pulley network. He pulled her effortlessly out of the foreboding chamber and down a long corridor, Liz swinging helplessly in her cage until he came to a large block of what could only be described as metal lockers. The dwarf went to one locker and opened its heavy door, then he threw some switches so that her cage was routed onto the pulley track which led to that open storage unit. He hauled again on the rope and the cage swung inside. It was featureless within, apart from a small air-conditioning vent and a grill on the floor, and was just about big enough to hold the cage.

Liz began to panic; surely she wasn't going to be shut away – filed away – in there!

The dwarf made some more adjustments and the cage transferred onto some small rails set in the ceiling of the locker, and he then pushed it deeper into the claustrophobic gloom within.

'Please…' Liz started, beginning to panic as the walls of the tiny locker engulfed her cramped cage.

'You stay in here until you're wanted again,' the dwarf gloated. 'It's soundproofed, so no one will hear you. If you're good I'll feed you later.'

'Wait – please wait!' she began, but the door shut with a heavy clunk to leave her in pitch darkness.

The cage swung gently with her movements as from her hunched position she peered around, but the gloom was impenetrable. Her back was already beginning to ache from its enforced posture and her thighs began to tremble. Carefully, she eased herself down onto the soles of her feet to ease the strain on her ankles, but that only increased the curvature of her back. Liz realised she would have to alternate her position when it became intolerable, to share out the burden of strain between her various cramped limbs. She had read about such contraptions in old history books of the Dark Ages. She believed they were called Little Ease, and she was now learning first hand just how they lived up to that name.

'Help... please, is anyone there?' she called out at the top of her voice, but only the deadened sound of her own words echoed back to her ears. There was no other sound, save the creaking of the suspended cage, and the subtle hiss of air being circulated. There was not a glimmer of light. Liz was totally alone and isolated. She began to cry. Commander Elizabeth Hartley, second-in-command of the most powerful space cruiser in the known worlds, squatted naked, confined in cramped silence and darkness within a tiny cage, awaiting whatever the pirates and their hoards of hideous dwarfs chose to do to her next.

Chapter Three

Mungo was pulling another cage towards its temporary resting-place in the prisoner storage rack – as the pirates called it. Whistling a tuneless song, he was happy in his work. Although good with his hands, Mungo wasn't burdened with a surfeit of intelligence, and it constantly amazed him how the rack of lockers could hold so many individuals. At times he had known over one hundred Federation prisoners to be confined there for various crimes. All were within centimetres of each other, and all were in total isolation and darkness within their tiny cages. They would be suffering and, after his uncaring treatment by the Federation, Mungo was very content to make it so. Many years before every Federation ship he had applied to for an engine room job had curtly turned him down and, when he had been tempted to steal in preference to starvation, he had languished in a prison for three months.

Mungo knew the Federation prisoners found him repulsive to look at, but he found it a positive advantage; it increased the discomfort of the charges he and his fellow dwarfs had to deal with, and he just loved that look of fear in their eyes. He glanced at the prisoner in the cage he was pulling now.

Helen Swale was tall, blonde, and voluptuous,

making her folded confinement even more difficult for her to bear. She had been one of *Explorer's* officers, and her high level of intelligence and quick brain had destined her to be head of the ship's vast computer banks. Unfortunately for her she spoke in a cultured manner, and was therefore the sort of person Mungo figured would normally not even spare him a cursory glance.

The naked flesh of her buttocks squashed against the bars made an irresistible target, and he cruelly pinched it so that lieutenant Helen Swale screeched with pain and outrage, but was quite unable to move away. Then he reached into the cage and grabbed a handful of her long blonde hair, pulling sharply.

'You're a fat pig,' he lied, cruelly poking her large breasts. 'But you'll get thinner in the cage.' He laughed, banging the suspended cell against an open locker door.

It happened to be the locker next to where Liz was cocooned, and Mungo stopped to rub his hands over the stained and greasy bulge in his trousers at the thought of the commander. He decided to treat himself to another look at the beauty – definitely the best in this bunch, he thought. Possibly his feelings were due to her being in such a senior position, and yet now under his power. She had been in her cage for two hours, although he knew for her it would seem much longer. He decided to give her some food, relishing such control.

Liz's eyes darted upwards at a faint sound. It was the

first sound she'd heard from beyond the sinister confinement since being shut in there. Was it hours ago? Her back and neck ached intolerably, her cramped muscles burned, and her thighs trembled because of their restriction of movement.

Suddenly light flooded in. Blinking furiously against the painful brightness, she saw the dwarf's hideous face haloed in the open doorway. There was no space to shrink back away from him – but did she really want to? Hideous though he was, he could let her out into the world of sound and light again if he chose to. Please let him choose to, she hoped desperately.

Mungo decided instead to slowly rotate his prisoner's cage so he could again view her beauty from every angle. He halted the movement with her back to him, and try as she might, he saw that she couldn't quite turn her head around to watch what he was up to. He savoured the sight of her curvaceous back, down to the graceful swell of her buttocks. He trailed a long finger between the bars to prod a cheek of her bottom, delighting in the way she jumped slightly. Then the finger moved slowly into the cool shadowy cleft.

'No... please...'

He loved the way she winced and begged as he pushed slightly against the enticing resistance of the entrance to her dark passage.

'You've got a nice arse,' he pondered, finally withdrawing and spinning her around again to face him. 'Take food and drink,' he said, thrusting two capsules of space rations through the bars.

Liz shuddered in disgust as she accepted the tablets from the fingers that had just been probing her anus, but she was realistic enough not to refuse the sustenance. She could have cried again as the door began to swing shut, but as it did she just noticed for the first time her junior officer, Helen Swale. They just managed to smile brief encouragement to each other. Then Liz's door shut and, once more, she was totally alone in the dark without a sound penetrating her little prison.

Time passed so slowly in her isolation. The muscles of her calves and thighs were knots screaming for release as she squatted. The cage was too small for her to sit. With white knuckles she gripped the closely set bars in her pain. If only she could have squeezed her legs or arms between them to give her more space, but it was impossible.

The soft hum of the air-conditioning was her only companion.

Chapter Four

The door of the locker crashing open wrenched Liz from her restless dozing. She looked hopefully at the dwarf as he immediately proceeded to pull her cage out.

'More questions for you,' was his only comment as he began tugging her back along the corridor.

Liz decided that whatever was now in store for her couldn't be much worse than the pain from her tortured muscles in this endless stooping cramp. As the cage swung on its chain she had another view of the banks of lockers. They looked so practical, so innocent. The casual observer would have no idea of the misery those soundproofed doors concealed; little individual boxes of muscle-burning agony.

As the cage rotated again Liz saw two other cages being pulled along, each by a dwarf. Mungo and the other dwarfs pointed at their mouths and waved their fists at their confined charges to emphasise that they were to remain silent while their captors briefly chatted. One cage contained the young crewman Kirk, and in the other was Cathy Flanders. Cathy was a non-commissioned officer and the oldest female member of Liz's crew. However, despite being in her early forties, her dark hair framed a very attractive face and

48

her body was still extremely fit and toned.

Liz cringed and tried to avert her eyes from poor blushing Kirk, as his penis, initially nestling limply between his thighs, was slowly stirring, no doubt influenced by the close proximity of two naked women.

Despite her awful predicament, the sight of the semi-erect penis had Liz briefly wondering about Harry's fate. Was he being questioned by that ogre Stern? Were her lifeless eyes consuming his fine body? Or perhaps he was crouched in a tiny cage within a locker. Maybe he'd been next to hers. A twinge of muscle cramp forced Liz to squeeze her eyes shut, and by the time she opened them she could see that her destination was a similar foreboding chamber to the one before. It appeared to be empty.

'Please, I'm too stiff,' began Liz, as the dwarf unlocked the cage door. 'I can't—' she yelped as, unsympathetic to her locked muscles, he simply scooped her compressed nudity and pulled her out. Oblivious to anything but the immediate need to at last stretch to full height again, Liz hardly noticed Mungo's lopsided leer as he watched while she pushed her fists into the hollow of her back, stretching up on tiptoe. She gave thanks that at least she and the other crewmembers were sufficiently physically fit to withstand such treatment without lasting harm.

With a hard slap across the rounded softness of her bottom, Liz was once again manhandled by the dwarf. He even grabbed her nose in a painful pinch to lead her like a naughty child to the position he required. Tears of pain and humiliation sprang to her eyes. She knew resistance was useless, and so she allowed him to bind her wrists to a pulley above her head and her ankles wide apart to ringbolts set in the floor. He then pulled her wrists up on the pulley until she was standing, legs astride, stretched up on tiptoe. Liz looked down apprehensively as he positioned a contraption between her legs, consisting of two short vertical metal poles with a third suspended horizontally between them. Adjusting the poles, he ensured the horizontal rod was high enough to brush against her delicate sex lips. She could just avoid contact with it by straining to the very tips of her toes, but as soon as she relaxed her quivering legs, the rod nestled uncomfortably into the softness of her sex again.

Methodically, her small tormentor pulled up a high stool, set it beside her and climbed onto it so he was level with her, face to face. Liz saw that the dwarf held a pair of blacked-out goggles, but her attention was soon directed to her breasts when the brute suddenly, eagerly, reached out and tweaked each red bud between his clammy fingers and twisted painfully.

'Ahhh… please,' she sobbed.

'Lovely…' the dwarf sighed as he lifted and mauled in his hairy hands the smooth, beautifully shaped orbs at his mercy. He giggled as he pushed his thumbs hard against her nipples, squashing them into the yielding flesh. Liz gasped, quite unable to flinch back more than a few centimetres. But then a noise from outside concentrated the dwarf's mind again. Quickly, he left her breasts alone and slipped the goggles over her eyes, rendering her quite blind. Liz heard the stool being moved away and then a different male voice in the room.

'Ah, Elizabeth Hartley, I see…' he chuckled, 'even if you cannot see me.

'I am Zuke, but you will call me, sir. I am sorry to subject you to more discomfort, but I'm afraid some of the answers you gave my associate, Stern, didn't quite tally with those of your crew, and I shall therefore need to delve a little further.

Zuke smiled at the sight of the beautiful naked girl, straining up on her toes, legs immodestly wide, her head questing blindly in the direction of his voice, almost bug-like and comical under her large black goggles. Her beauty was in stark contrast to the squat ugliness of the little mutant who stood by her flank and who, he could tell by the pink marks on her smooth breasts, had just given her what was almost certainly an unpleasant mauling.

Zuke turned at a sound behind him and smiled again as another cage was brought in on a pulley by another dwarf. It contained the naked and gagged figure of Harry Clarke, the captain of the enemy ship *Explorer*, who started in helpless fury at the unmistakable sight of his helpless second-in-command. If the information from that bumbling oaf McDuff and one or two others was correct, the captain knew his second-in-command rather well.

Harry's confinement was even more restrictive than Liz's by virtue of his wrists being strapped behind him so that he was unable to remove his gag. This also meant, of course, that he could not pull on the bars to ease his position. Instead, his weight rested either on his head or his back. He would have dearly loved to wrench the door off the cage and strangle the disgusting dwarfs and the smirking figure of Zuke, but he could only watch in tormented silence as the evil pirate turned again to address Liz.

'As I say, we need to go over some of your previous answers, Hartley. And if there is any hesitation on your part, or attempts to mislead us, the rod between your pretty legs will be heated within a fraction of a second. It cools just as rapidly when I switch it off, but of course, if you are reticent it may remain hot for some time. Additionally, your friend Mungo has quite a thin cane in his grasp, which he will apply to your rather splendid backside.

'So firstly, the customary demonstration…'

Liz's cries gradually increased in intensity as Zuke's fingers moved to a switch on a console by his side and the rod became hot. Although not red hot, it was enough to make her want to put even more strain on her aching toes to keep her soft lips and sensitive flesh away from it. Even then, at absolutely full stretch, she could feel the threatening heat.

Harry's restrained hands were fists of helpless fury

as he saw Liz straining to the very tips of her toes, muscles knotted in her thighs, her body as taut as a bow-string. He bit down harder on the gag as Zuke casually strolled over to her, idly trailing his fingertips lightly over her straining thighs, the unexpected contact making her jump. The swine then turned briefly to give Harry a broad, man-to-man wink, before patting Liz's magnificent clenched bottom. He then removed his hand and nodded at the dwarf.

Whack!

Liz shrieked as the cane lashed down across both buttocks to leave a line of burning agony. The pain was enhanced when she squirmed, only for her exposed sex to come into contact with the hot pole, sending her arching back up again onto her toes.

Whack!

Liz shrieked again and tossed her head from side to side, trying desperately to deny the scorching and undeserved pain.

The dwarf giggled, clearly enjoying himself immensely.

Instead of watching the tortured writhing of the beautiful girl, Zuke looked from the corner of his eye at Harry, watching for the reactions that would confirm the information he'd been offered gladly by McDuff, and had extracted without too much difficulty from one or two of the other crewmembers. Happy that the information was correct, he turned off the switch and nodded to the dwarf, who lowered the cane until its tip touched the floor and it was no longer a threat.

Harry gave silent thanks when Liz was able to sink back very slightly onto the balls of her feet, the rod just a warm glow lying between her thighs.

'Hmm, nice upholstery,' Zuke smirked, with another wink at Harry as he again stroked the rounded contours of Liz's pert bottom, a finger tracing over the twin weals left by the cane, making her flinch again. 'Even if it is slightly damaged, now. But if you're a good girl your bottom will still be just as beautiful when we've done – and if not…'

'Look, please, I've answered your questions,' Liz pleaded. 'I've nothing else to *say*!' Liz's rebellion ended in an arched-back squeal as, simultaneously, the pole became hot between her legs and the cane lifted and lashed down across her buttocks to create another line of excruciating pain.

Zuke switched off the pole after around thirty seconds of Liz desperately straining up on tiptoe. Then she subsided as far as she was able, gasping for breath, her chin resting on her heaving chest.

'Two errors, Hartley,' Zuke continued matter-of-factly as if nothing had happened; as if he hadn't just been responsible for inflicting agony on a his helpless captive. 'You spoke out of turn, and you omitted to call me, sir.

'Now, do you want a repeat performance, or shall we go over the questions again?'

'No… no sir,' Liz conceded wearily. 'I'll answer any

questions you have.'

She just wanted the ordeal to be over. She knew they could keep on hurting and humiliating her until she cracked and told them everything anyway. And it seemed some of the other crewmembers had already given way and told the pirates whatever they wanted to know, so it would be foolish for her to suffer unnecessarily; if an escape was to be successfully instigated she would need to conserve every ounce of strength and keep her wits about her. She would have to fall in line; she could no longer afford to hold back, to be out of step with the others.

'Now, Hartley, you previously gave the maximum speed of *Explorer* as five mega-pecs, but this conflicts with other statements. Tell me again, what is its maximum?'

'Eight megas... sir,' Liz responded hesitantly to the anonymous voice from the darkness.

'Good, that tallies.' Zuke circled her slowly, his astute eyes studying her closely. 'Now, when will the next ship of this class be built on Earth?'

'I... I think another two years... sir.'

'Hmm, better than your previous answer of no more due to be built, but just think a little harder, if you please...'

Liz shrieked again, arching forward as the awful heat burst between her legs.

'Okay... okay,' she panted, her breasts rising and falling as she breathed deeply. 'It – it m-might be one year… s-sir.' What did it matter? thought Liz bitterly; they obviously had the correct version from elsewhere.

'Good, that's better,' the torturer continued casually. 'I hope you appreciate that with only a little persuasion – far less than you've chosen to endure – your former captain was most forthcoming, furnishing us with much of what we wanted to know.'

Liz had sufficient faith in Harry not to believe he would easily crack, but then, he was only flesh and blood. And in any case, between them most of the other officers knew collectively as much as he did. The thought of Harry brought tears to her eyes under the goggles. Was he safe? Would she ever see him again?

Harry, just a few metres away, his fists balled in impotent fury, saw Zuke croon over the sobbing Liz. His hands were around her shaking shoulders, stroking. He lifted her chin and kissed her lips, murmuring softly as if he genuinely cared for her wellbeing.

The questions continued and Liz's answers flowed. Then, as with Stern, the personal questions arose. Obviously the crew had not held back in that area either.

'How long have you been the lover of Clarke?'

'I… we...' her shoulders slumped in resignation. 'About two years, sir,' she answered quietly.

'And do you love him?'

'Yes, sir, I do.'

Harry's heart went out to her.

'So how often do you find the time and privacy to be intimate with each other in, say, an average month?'

Liz flinched visibly at the shock of such a question. 'Please sir, why?'

'Do you want more of the hot rod?' Zuke asked, almost conversationally. 'As I say, Clarke has been extremely forthcoming – boasting, you might even say, like men from Earth naturally do. So think carefully before answering me. How often?'

'It – it's not that often... sir. We're in space for long periods. Perhaps... perhaps every landfall we...'

'Think, Hartley, and be honest,' Zuke insisted, wanting to squeeze every last drop of humiliation from his prisoner, and in front of her mute lover, too. He was also finding her futile resistance to this sudden line of intimate questioning rather a turn on. 'On average, how many times in a month?'

'About... about twice a month, sir,' she whispered. She just wanted the floor to swallow her up, wanted the tormenting voice to stop, to leave her in peace.

'Good.' Zuke's inscrutable smile widened a little. Then he moved closer again and, with another wink at the hapless captain, he moved the rod from between Liz's thighs and placed his cupped hand over her pubic mound. 'Is he as clever as this?' he asked casually.

She gasped, quite unable to flinch away as she felt two strong fingers rub gently over her sex lips.

'There, I'll make you feel better.' He spoke softly in her ear, and then kissed her gently.

Liz's moist lips peeled apart beneath the feather-light kiss, and she sighed involuntarily as the experienced fingers found her clitoris and gently teased it. She quivered slightly as the fingers slid up into her, the thumb flicking her now engorged bud. The kiss ended, and then the lips fluttered down her throat, over the upper sweep of her breasts, into her cleavage, and then fastened onto her right nipple, sucking in the treacherously erect bud. Teeth nipped gently.

Zuke released the nipple and regarded the beautiful naked girl, her hips gently undulating under his moving fingers, trying to absorb more of them into her enticing softness. Her mouth was open and inviting, her head thrown back, the tendons taut in her neck, as she struggled against the conflicting pain of stretching on tiptoe and the delights his fingers were evoking.

'I think I'll let you enjoy an orgasm, my dear,' he murmured hypnotically. 'You've had a pretty rough ride.'

'Yes, please...' she gasped urgently, hating herself but unable to resist. Zuke turned to give Harry another sly smile as his fingers worked on the panting girl, her hips now grinding in hopeless abandon against his hand, gyrating around the fingers that were currently the centre of her universe. Her shapely buttocks clenched, opened and contracted under his ministrations.

'Yeah, I bet this is better than anything you ever got from him, isn't it?' he taunted. 'Or shall I stop now?'

'No, oh please no, don't stop,' she begged hopelessly. 'Yes... yes, it's better.' Shame engulfed Liz, for the pleasure she was relishing, elevating her above the awfulness of her situation for a few brief moments, was too strong to prevent her betraying Harry's trust and love. All she knew, through colliding emotions, was that she needed those teasing fingers to give her the release she desperately craved; needed the release they were giving after the tension of her ordeal.

Thankfully, with mouth open and head thrown back, long hair cascading down her slender back, Liz gasped to a shuddering climax.

Zuke watched his fingers within her liquid womanhood, heard the erotic squelching as they moved, felt her muscles gripping, holding, before gently relaxing as her passion slowly subsided.

After a little while longer, as Liz slumped as far as the bonds would allow, Zuke withdrew his glistening fingers from her heat. Smirking evilly and turning to Harry's cage, Zuke held the fingers under his nose and his nostrils flared as he made a great show of savouring her scent, as though he was anticipating the joys of a quality cigar before lighting it. Then he walked over to his male captive.

'Hmm,' he cooed softly so only Harry could hear, and then pushed his fingers through the bars under Harry's nose.

'Well, well,' he said smugly, when he noticed the partially erect penis pulsing between the thighs of the squatting prisoner. 'So you enjoyed her little performance too?' He sneered. 'You know, I really do despise the lack of willpower you people from Earth display. And yet you think yourselves so superior. Well, not for very much longer, my dear captain – I can assure you of that. Times are changing.'

And perhaps Zuke wasn't wrong about willpower. Although Harry would have done anything to prevent the bastard from handling Liz in such a flagrant and abusive way, he could not deny the excitement he felt at witnessing his lover in the throes of her orgasm. He jerked back the few centimetres his confinement would allow, but was unable to prevent Zuke's moistened fingers from reaching down through the bars and curling around his stiffening penis. The hand slid up and down, slowly massaging Liz's juices into the absorbent column of flesh. Harry groaned with utter shame, for he couldn't prevent his erection from swelling further beneath the vile touch of the other man. He closed his eyes and bit down on the gag, fighting against the approaching orgasm that would humiliate him almost beyond endurance. Despite the unthinkable degradation of being masturbated by one of his most loathed enemy – and a male enemy, at that – Harry could feel his orgasm building rapidly. He tried desperately to fight it, but Zuke egged him on, whispering words of encouragement. Saliva built up around the gag as he tried miserably to ignore the undeniably delicious sensations building in his groin. The speed and tightness of the gripping fist increased, the ball of a thumb knowingly teased the underside of his helmet, and Harry could do nothing but give in to the pleasure. He opened his eyes and did his utmost to throw a challenging stare at the smirking Zuke as he groaned into the gag and erupted over the wrist of his loathsome tormentor. His hips jerked and he spurted again.

As soon as his ejaculations lessened he was swamped with self-retribution. How could he have been so weak? How had he allowed himself to be so utterly humiliated by his enemy, with one of the despicable mutants watching?

As Harry slumped in despair, Zuke dropped the sticky penis as though it disgusted him, took a tissue from a pocket, wiped his hand with disdain, and discarded the soggy paper in the bottom of Harry's cage, leaving it there as a graphic reminder of his little victory. With a triumphant snort of derision Zuke looked at Harry's rapidly wilting manhood, and then turned his attention back to Liz.

'Back to your cage now, my pretty one,' he said. 'You're a deliciously randy little tart, and I just know we're going to have a lot more fun with you.' He laughed, knowing Harry would have heard the remark before the dwarf pulled his cage out of the chamber. He then nodded for Mungo to take care of Liz, and left the chamber himself.

Liz felt totally ashamed of her performance under the fingers of the unknown interrogator, and of the traitorous things she had said.

When Mungo had restored her sight by pulling off the goggles, leaving her blinking in the unaccustomed light, he smirked at her, patting her bottom. 'You're hot, eh?' Without awaiting any kind of response he pressed a clammy hand into the humid warmth between her spread thighs.

She cringed under the wretched fingers as he removed her bonds, and so despicable did she find him, was almost thankful to be squeezed back into the tiny cage.

Out of the chamber and back in the gloomy corridors, they passed another cage of human misery, presumably on its way for questioning. Liz was unable to meet the eyes of the occupant, and tears meandered down her cheeks. She knew that by succumbing so easily to the pirate she had betrayed herself, Harry, and the crew who counted on her. And she had no idea who the man was who had opprobriously broken her will.

The all-embracing darkness and solitude of the locker, after the door had banged shut on her, allowed her to sob freely in her shame.

Chapter Five

Liz didn't know how long she was in the locker. She drifted in and out of an uncomfortable sleep, woken at intervals by the searing pain in her cramped muscles, changing position as much as the bars would allow and then drifting off to an uncomfortable sleep again. In her more lucid moments she wondered what was happening to the others, especially Harry, and what would become of them all.

The sound of a key turning in the lock startled her into awareness, and the door opened to once again allow her to rejoin the world outside her contorted isolation. The dwarf pulled her cage out of the locker without comment and towed it behind him the short distance to the room where she had first been questioned.

Stern was seated at a desk, and she remained perusing some papers while the dwarf unlocked the cage door and pulled Liz's aching body from its confinement. To her surprise, after she had carefully straightened her limbs, she was not bound again, but was manhandled by the dwarf until she stood before Stern's desk.

'Hands on head please, Hartley,' Stern ordered without looking up, knowing that the dwarf would ensure she obeyed. 'Remain silent and still.'

Minutes ticked away while Liz waited anxiously.

Only the occasional rustle of papers broke the silence as the woman flicked through them, seemingly oblivious to the beauty standing before her. Liz remained staring ahead, but conscious of the dwarf prowling about behind her.

Indeed, Mungo was once again drinking in the delicious succulence of the girl's body, his hand automatically straying to the pocket of his grubby trousers, feeling the throbbing hardness there. He and the other pirates were normally allowed to 'use' the females when they had been drained of useful information, and he had particularly asked for this one in view of her exceptional beauty. As, by luck of the draw, he had been responsible for fetching her to and from the lockers he had been told that she would eventually be his plaything. His limited imagination was already working overtime as he contemplated having her to himself. Until recently she had been the second-in-command of a powerful space ship from the planet Earth, an intelligent woman in charge of incredibly expensive high-tech equipment and many members of crew. Here though, she was simply a delicious specimen who would have to do his bidding. He wiped a sliver of spittle from his chin as he drank in the elegant beauty. Then Stern interrupted his perverse fantasising.

'Well, Hartley, I am afraid you have caused us much trouble.' The unattractive woman fixed her captive with an icy stare over her glasses. 'Firstly, in destroying so many of our ships and crew, for which you as an officer must take responsibility, and secondly for being evasive and rather economical with the truth during your questioning.'

Stern held up a hand and resumed her tirade as Liz opened her mouth to try to interject. 'Silence, or Mungo will punish you severely,' she said firmly. 'I am not interested in excuses, or any of this whining about you being merely soldiers and our planets being at war with each other. You have roamed around these regions, delighting in trying to subdue us from the safety of your ship with your fancy computers, weapons and technology. But now you are here before us without the protection of your ship, and it is time for you and your fellow officers to pay the necessary price; to atone for your oppressive actions.'

Stern lifted a casket from the floor at her feet. Feeling sick to the stomach, Liz saw it contained some of her personal items from her cabin on *Explorer*.

'Interesting personal effects,' Stern pondered, extracting some and placing them on her desk. Liz's heart sank as her treasured possessions, each bringing back its own fond memories, were coldly examined and picked over.

Books, for instance, which she would cuddle up with and retreat into alone in her cabin at night. Many had been given to her in tender circumstances, contrasting so vividly with the present reality.

The 3D vid-discs, her personal vid-player, photos,

intimate clothing, all were carelessly discarded across the desktop. Liz felt her innermost secrets had been laid bare. Elegant and sexy dresses, underwear she had expected only Harry would ever see, were all held up for ridicule before being ritually screwed into balls and dismissively thrown into a corner.

'Hmm, you've expensive taste in perfume, Hartley,' Stern sneered, spraying some behind her rather large ears. 'Shame to let such lovely fragrances go to waste.' She put the tiny phials in her desk drawer, the beautiful scent contrasting with the permeating stench of fear ingrained in the surrounding grey metal walls.

A feeling of sheer hopelessness swamped Liz as she watched Stern sweep the remaining articles back into the casket. Her life had been swept away – taken from her.

But she was very wrong if she thought she had yet hit rock bottom.

'And this was a decidedly interesting little item we found hidden in your former captain's cabin,' Stern sneered, standing up, holding a hologram.

Liz felt disgusted as Stern and the dwarf gloated over the nude picture of her, which Harry had taken some time before. She was in a revealing pose, pouting her charms below the invitation in her wide brown eyes. It was intended for his eyes only, and it's exposure before these hideous creeps made her feel nauseous. She began to weep, her hands covering her pale drawn face.

'Keep your hands on your head,' Stern reprimanded

as the dwarf pulled her back into position.

Stern put the hologram on the desk and licked her lips as her eyes roamed over the exquisite beauty before her. She walked slowly around the desk and reached out with a thin hand, luxuriating in the feel of her captive flinching away as she stroked her fingertips over the soft warmth of one perfect breast, the nipple stiffening under her touch. She gently weighed the flesh in her palm, lifting and examining. Her other hand gently stroked Liz's neck, delighting in the girl's sickened expression as her fingertips trailed down her spine to stroke the satin cheeks of her bottom.

'Mmm, you really are a very lovely young lady, my dear. Maybe we shall meet again after you've been punished.'

Liz sighed with relief as the hands left her. 'W-what are you going to do with us—?'

Whack!

Liz cried out as the dwarf's vicious hand slapped across her bottom, leaving a red swathe of pain in its wake. Such was the hardness and strength of his hand that Liz rocked forward slightly on her toes.

'You do not speak without prior permission, Hartley!' Stern scolded, and then her expression immediately softened a little. 'But on this occasion I will explain… whilst on the way to your first trial. Firstly, though, you may dress.'

Liz glanced hopefully towards her personal clothing from *Explorer*, but Stern laughed, shaking her head.

'Oh no, my dear. You left such choices behind when you attacked us. You can wear this.' She took a bundle of red material from another of the desk's drawers and threw it at Liz. It was a one-piece suit. 'Hurry girl, put it on – or go naked.'

Cringing before the virulent dwarf and the cold-eyed woman, and mustering as much dignity as she could, Liz squeezed with some difficulty into the tight garment. Tailored from thin latex which clung to every contour like a second skin, it was designed to titillate. The outline of her nipples, strangely aroused by the rubber's warm caress, clearly protruded. The cheeks of her buttocks moved with visible definition when Stern had Liz walk up and down a couple of times. Her body flowed gracefully under the material, while the dwarf clapped and giggled like a spoilt child. It was an outrageous garment she would never have dared to wear at home.

Then the dwarf cuffed her wrists together behind her back.

'Open,' he demanded, reaching up to prod her lips, and Liz was subjected to the discomfort of having a ball gag pushed unceremoniously into her mouth and strapped extremely tightly around her head.

'There, we're all ready now,' Stern said, like a parent having readied a child to go out for the day. She fastened a narrow collar and thin metal chain around Liz's slender throat, and then patted her bottom with a familiarity that made Liz's skin crawl.

'Come along then.' Stern tugged the breathtakingly sensual rubber figure. 'I'll explain about your endurance tests of contrition on the way.'

They left the room, Stern's footsteps clacking on the metallic floors of the seemingly endless corridors while Liz's bare feet padded softly along behind.

'You see,' Stern started to explain over her shoulder as they walked in convoy, 'we have from you and the others all we want, but we have to take account of our people's popular opinion.'

Stern stopped walking for a moment and pulled Liz into a small shadowy recess. The bound girl was unable to flinch back as Stern pulled her softness against her. Her breasts, tummy and thighs beneath the clinging latex crushed against Stern's wiry form within the crisp white coat. Stern's bony hands stroked over Liz's shoulders and down her spine while she continued, their lips almost touching.

'We are both intelligent women, and you must realise that, although we are both professionals, the lesser inhabitants of this planet demand to see their aggressors punished; to see justice done. We are perhaps not as barbaric as the reputation we like to project; we are just a people who want independence from the Federation.

'However, the ordinary people here, the people who support us, have suffered because of your ship, and it is necessary that they see the perpetrators of such suffering, suffer themselves.'

She smiled, but with little sincerity. 'There is nothing personal in this, and the fact that I find you such a gorgeous creature who looks intoxicating when suffering has absolutely nothing to do with it.' As if to emphasise the fact that she found Liz deeply desirable, she squeezed the firm ripe fruit of Liz's bottom, making the lush beauty squirm uncomfortably.

'You realise, I trust, that we have to make an example of some of you, especially the officers, for the benefit of our people. All of your interrogations have been filmed, and extracts will be shown to them.

'However, you will also go through endurance tests, as will some of the others, which will again be filmed for the benefit of the people. The only person who will be spared, for the moment, is your former captain. In an altruistic gesture to counter common misconceptions that exist beyond our empire, and prove we are not barbarians, we will offer some regard for his rank.' She peered intently at Liz, and the hands continued to maul, the fingers probing into the deep valley between the succulent buttocks. 'But that is where you come in, my dear.'

Liz felt sick, and didn't really want to know any more.

'You, as the next most senior officer, will be undertaking the endurance tests on his behalf. However, if you refuse to undergo them properly, or you fail to complete them, then not only will you of course suffer, but so will your entire crew and former captain.

'Please then, be very clear about this, my dear. Not

only your life, but also those of *all* your crew, will depend on your obedience and your ability. If you fail to comply there will be regularly filmed executions until you change your mind, with the blame being clearly attributed to yourself. So, my pretty, the fate of so many depends upon you… and you alone.' Stern smiled, and lifted a hand to gently pat Liz's soft cheek, slightly distended around the gag.

'Many of you may come through all of this and then, when public opinion has been satisfied, we might be able to bargain and exchange you for something worthwhile…' her dry lips brushed against the cornered beauty's, '…although you I would like to keep.' She sighed, her stale breath sickening Liz.

Stern suddenly snaked her fingers into Liz's hair and kissed her hard. Liz tried to protest, but she was squashed into the dark corner and it was hopeless.

Eventually the kiss ended and Stern sighed again, gazing into her gorgeous victim's eyes, and her hands again cupped and pulled her rubber-clad bottom, urgently crushing their groins together, feeling the delicious girl squirm futilely against her.

'Hmm… you really are delicious,' she breathed, and then abruptly broke away. 'But we'd better go now, before they send out a search party.'

Stern adjusted the collar of her uniform, patted her lifeless hair into place and, with a sharp jerk, continued to lead her dazed captive through the maze of gloomy humming corridors.

They passed some large cells containing several members of *Explorer's* crew. In marked contrast to the others she had seen being transported in those suspended cages, they were dressed in space coveralls and appeared to have been well treated. Liz caught the eye of McDuff who, with a sickly grin, moved over to the bars, licking his lips and openly drinking in the sheen of Liz's polished curves.

'These crewmembers were more co-operative than the others,' explained Stern, 'and so they are receiving better treatment.'

'Good morning, commander,' McDuff said mockingly, his eyes crawling slowly over her splendid figure, and then back up to Liz's angry eyes above the gag. 'I hope you're enjoying yourself,' he smirked.

'She has not been as co-operative as we'd hoped, and she does have a certain responsibility for *Explorer's* activities in the area, McDuff,' Stern replied for Liz, 'so her stay will not be as comfortable as yours, I'm afraid.'

'Oh, I *am* sorry to hear that,' McDuff chuckled. Without taking his loathsome stare from Liz he lazily rubbed the disgusting bulge in his trousers and addressed Stern. 'I'm sure, if you gave me a few hours alone with my, *commander*, I could make her considerably more co-operative for you,' he sneered.

Liz couldn't understand what she'd ever done to make the man hate her so much.

'That will not be necessary,' Stern snorted, and then

72

whis___ on the leash and she was unceremoniously ___ to her. ___ her shoulder she heard McDuff wolf-___ ___ crudely on what he'd gladly do

And Liz was fille___ ___ premonition that one day M___ inexplicable and dreadful his perverted ambitions. ___ ___ might get to fulfil

Chapter Six

Liz found herself ~~turned~~ into in a narrow cylindrical cell about five metres in height. It had smooth metal walls, unbroken ap~~ar~~t from a largish grill set about two metres up. St~~ern~~ took off the prisoner's collar and leash, and re~~pl~~aced it with another collar studded with buttons. For some reason she touched it with obvious respect, and carefully adjusted it.

'Two hours should do it,' Stern muttered to herself, pressing some of the buttons. She stood back and studied Liz, who was still gagged and still had her wrists fastened behind her back.

'The collar will start to contract in two hours, until it deprives you of oxygen, my pretty,' Stern suddenly announced, casually. 'That is how long you have to complete the obstacle course and find me. It will beep with increasing frequency as your time limit approaches.'

The hateful woman smiled at the expression of horror that froze Liz's features. 'It can only be deactivated by my code, and I shall be somewhere at the end of this first course – assuming you complete it. Naturally, I will now unfasten your wrists and remove the gag, and I don't think we'll bother with clothing. A person naked, just using their courage and wits, faces far more of a

...ge, I always find.'

'...dicated that Liz should turn around, and the
want you ...aved from her wrists.

Liz hated the ...it off, my precious,' she ordered. 'I
...nded.'

humiliation, but soon s... was subjecting her to such
garment in Stern's wa... the gleaming rubber
automatically covered her bare ...nds. Her arms
the heartless eyes. ...asts and sex from

'I'm sure you can unfasten the gag your...lf,' Stern
added. 'I'll leave now; I expect you'll want to start the
course as soon as you can. You now have one hour and
fifty-six minutes left.' She slipped out and locked the
door behind her, as Liz struggled to get some feeling
back into her fingertips and unbuckle the strap of the
gag from behind her head.

She looked around her tiny metal prison, wondering
just what was expected of her, but the cell was
featureless apart from the grill. Suddenly the lights
dimmed to a faint eerie red glow, and Liz's stomach
sank as she heard a gurgling from below the floor and
the terrifying sound of rushing water. She could only
just make out her bare feet in the dim red light but then,
as she looked, a recessed panel at floor level slid back
and cold water began cascading in.

Liz gasped with shock and dread as the icy water
bubbled around her. In no time the remorseless tide
swirled up to her knees with no sign of abating.

Desperately looking around in the dim ...tery
that the only possible hope of esc... ...ected by
grave seemed to be through the ... ...and lifted her
the grill. She jumped up to ... ...ing herself up she
feet clear of the numbing ... entrance to the conduit
peered into the dark for... ...last place in the world she
beyond the grill. It ... ...she felt the water lapping at
wanted to enter ... the ... held onto the edge. Looking
her flailing feet as ... ...reflected dully on the steadily rising
down, the red li... ...and she knew she had no choice but to
froth of w...er, ...try and get into that tunnel, or drown where she was.

Resting her weight on one elbow, Liz hooked her fingers into the tough plastic of the grill and pulled. It moved a little, giving her hope but not sanctuary. She realised she would have to use her full weight and the strength of two hands. Carefully bringing her knees up so they rested on the wall just below the conduit entrance, she hooked her fingers into the grill and, arching her back and pushing with her knees, she tugged desperately.

The grill moved, it creaked, but it held. While drawing a deep breath and resting for a moment, the grill cut agonisingly into her fingers. But she clung on bravely. The rising water, blood red in the reflection from the indistinct light, was not far below the taut curve of her bottom, lapping around her toes. She knew she just had to pull that grill out. With muscles and sinews straining she arched back again, teeth clenched, eyes closed,

pulling and jerking with her entire weight. W
wrenching crash, partially drowned by the echoi...
the water, the grill burst free from its fixings. Liz and
the broken plastic tumbled backwards into the icy
whirling water.

Initially panicking as she was totally submerged, she
then felt the metal floor beneath her feet and managed
to stand. The water churned just below her goose-
pimpled breasts. With a desperate lunge, the suction of
the water trying to hold her down, Liz just managed to
again grasp the lip of the entrance to the conduit. She
strained up on cold muscles to haul herself slowly into
the threatening darkness of the tunnel. She flopped,
gasping and shivering, her bare shoulders and hips
touching the cold rounded wall.

She lay for a few moments, collecting her thoughts
and her breath. Without thinking she had hooked the
strap of the gag over her wrist and that, and a torn
section of the grill, were with her in the tunnel. She
began to discard them but then stopped; being naked,
any object she had with her might be of some use for
whatever lay ahead.

Then, to her horror, she felt the icy trickle of water
licking around her feet and ankles. She had to move
fast to escape it, or drown in her metal coffin!

Slithering along like a snake, she tried to shut her
mind from whatever horrors might lay ahead in the
engulfing darkness. The pursuing water was getting
deeper around her. In the claustrophobic tunnel there

was just the sound of her rasping breath, her slithering and splashing movements on the metal, and the rushing water. Now only able to keep her chin above it, she was beginning to panic in the confining darkness.

As it reached her mouth, Liz had to incline her head upward to gulp in each breath. But that was only a brief respite, for soon her nose, her eyes, and then her face was submerged. Liz was a fighter, but as the bubbles echoed in her ears and her lungs burned for oxygen, she gave up. Stern had won, and this was to be Liz Hartley's ignominious end; drowned in a dark metal tunnel like a rat caught in a flooding sewer. She lay still in her watery tomb, using her last ounce of breath to say goodbye to Harry, when the running water carried her along a little and her extended hands felt an upward turn of the tunnel!

Sobbing with thanks she reacted instantly and hauled herself round the bend. She sat, retching water and trying to fill her aching lungs with cool air. Dizziness overwhelmed her and she rested her head against the metal tunnel, which now rose vertically. But with returning desperation she realised the water was still rising and was already up to her breasts, her legs completely submerged in the section of tunnel she'd thought was to be where she met her end.

She looked up into the dark void stretching above her. There was no indication of what might be up there, but there was no doubt she would have to climb up and find out.

Wearily, she pulled herself up by raising and pressing her arms and shoulders against the walls to support her weight. Inching up, before pressing her thighs against the wall to hold her, she reached above to repeat the process. It was excruciatingly difficult, but after a few metres she was, at last, well clear of the water. Bracing her shoulders, she allowed herself a few minutes to recover her breath and push the ever-present panic back deeper into her mind to prevent it from overwhelming her.

As her breathing calmed a little, Liz could hear more clearly the frightening pursuit of the unseen water in the darkness below, and it gave her the strength to continue. Eventually, on one upward thrust of her arms, she felt another horizontal tunnel leading off the vertical one, and she thankfully hauled herself into it, being careful not to lose her grip and plummet back down into the ever waiting water. She knew that would be the end; she wouldn't have the will or energy left to struggling against the icy grave again.

A few more minutes passed with Liz lying on her front, trying to collect her thoughts and her strength, but she was conscious of the collar about her neck and the need to somehow struggle on to get it released. She knew she'd passed the first test – but what other horrors lay ahead?

Chapter Seven

Harry was relieved to be released from the cramped confinement of his cage. However, he was uncomfortable at still only being allowed to wear the ridiculous baggy clothing, especially when taken into a rather more plush looking room than that in which he had been interrogated.

It was spacious with comfortable chairs, and Harry was allowed to ease himself into one. He was further surprised when one of the dwarfs served him a very nice cup of coffee. Then a door opened and a tall slim man entered.

The man smiled, causing his pencil thin moustache under a thin sharp nose to curve upwards, exposing gleaming white teeth.

'Welcome, Harry Clarke,' he said, in cultured tones. 'I am Valdez, chief executive of the Magellan empire. May I take this opportunity to apologise for the nature of your confinement, but for obvious reasons the Federation is not at all popular on Magellan.'

'I must protest most strongly,' said Harry, feeling that at last there just might be a flicker of light at the end of the tunnel. 'My crew have been treated despicably, and I demand humane treatment for them in accordance with the space charter for prisoners of war. I—'

'Not quite so fast, if you don't mind,' Va interrupted with disdain. 'Things can be made better vastly better – for you and your crew, but we first wish you to disable the self-destruct mechanisms on *Explorer*, which we've been told about by some members of your crew. Then we can use the ship ourselves, and may even use it to return your crew to Earth.'

Harry cursed inwardly that someone had blabbed about the destruct mechanisms, but he supposed it was inevitable. And the pirates definitely weren't fools. But he said, 'That's impossible. You cannot expect me to simply hand over our finest fighting ship to—'

'Think carefully before you make such rash decisions,' Valdez calmly interrupted again. 'Take time to think about it. You see, you seem to be forgetting a certain Elizabeth Hartley... Oh yes, I know you are more than a little close to her. We were told that you and she...' he smirked, 'well... I needn't spell it out for you – need I?

'Indeed, I appreciate your taste,' he continued, goading and watching for reactions. 'I've seen the film records of her interrogation, and I have to say she is a particularly lovely specimen.'

Valdez walked slowly around Harry, eyeing him closely. 'Well, I'm afraid your precious Liz is undergoing something of a nightmare as we speak.'

'If you so much as—' began Harry, trying to rise, but the dwarf pushed him contemptuously back into the seat.

'Pray let me continue, my dear captain – for her sake. Now, take a look up at those large ducts running below the ceiling.' He pointed up vaguely, without lifting his eyes from Harry.

'They look quite ordinary from here, don't they?' he continued, a glint of sadistic amusement in his narrowed eyes. 'But ordinary they most definitely are not. You see, within them is a nightmare world, and as you sit here enjoying our hospitality, your Liz is crawling naked through those very ducts, in total darkness, encountering all sorts of horrible things; rats, creepy-crawlies, freezing water.

'Just imagine her for a moment, crawling in the dark, naked, reaching out with tremulous hands, wondering what she'll encounter next, but informed that she must keep going and reach the end or a pretty little necklace she's wearing will choke the very life out of her. So on she goes, on her own little obstacle course.'

As Harry, ashen-faced, began to speak, Valdez turned dismissively and switched on a vid.

'In case you're wondering, Liz isn't the only one suffering. I'll find a record, at random, of another of your crewmembers.'

A huge screen flickered into life to show a pretty woman who Harry recognised as one of his crew. She stood stiffly naked, hands on head, before a sweating pirate. Casually, the pirate reached out to fondle one of her breasts. Harry was amazed when she didn't react aversely. The grimy fingers trailed lazily up th valley between her breasts, up over the pulse throat, and suggestively probed between her slightly parted lips. When the hand returned to her gently rising and falling breasts, she bravely nibbled her lower lip, but didn't otherwise react.

'When I did that before your interrogation you swore at me, if I recall correctly,' the pirate taunted.

'Yes, sir.' The lovely girl's response was a whisper; the self-control she had to exercise was obvious to all.

'Now what do you say, girl?'

'Th-thank you, s-sir, for touching me.' She parted with each word reluctantly.

The pirate made a lewd display of undressing, and then, with his erection bobbing between his thighs, he sneered, 'Now, what would you like me to do?'

'P-please, sir,' she stammered, closing her eyes against her tormentor. 'Please fuck me, sir.'

'On your back then, legs spread,' he ordered gruffly. 'And make it good, unless you want to go back in the cage…'

Valdez faded the picture as the slender woman, dark eyes flashing disgust and controlled hatred, lay back and accepted the gloating pirate's turgid column of flesh.

'My men take their job of eradicating any resistance very seriously,' Valdez explained smoothly, and then sniggered. 'You'll no doubt remember Zuke interrogating your Liz.'

Harry clenched his fists, silently craving the chance to wreak revenge on his enemy.

'Now, think about your predicament for a while, captain. Imagine what is happening to Liz. We have much more for her to endure while you contemplate your options and we examine the ship at our leisure. At some time in the near future I will ask you again about decommissioning the self-destruct. We may well discover how to disarm it without your help, but I gather the odds are against that. You may refuse to assist us, but I suggest you spare a thought for what will then happen to your crew... and particularly, your dear Elizabeth.'

Chapter Eight

Cold and wet, ~~Lucy~~ had been sliding along the tunnel on her breasts, belly and knees for several minutes, making fairly good progress but reluctant to surge ahead in the darkness without first blindly reaching out with her hands to check there was nothing untoward just ahead.

Then her questing ears detected the first sounds of shuffling and squeaking coming from ahead, and her pace slowed, her heart in her mouth.

The sounds grew louder as she cautiously inched forward. She stopped, holding her breath, watching and listening. Whatever was making the noise, they didn't seem to be coming for her. So, calling upon every ounce of courage, she eased forward again until her path was unexpectedly blocked by another thin mesh, similar to the one that had blocked the entrance to the horrific labyrinth. The squealing noises were on the other side of it.

She pulled back slightly. A dim yellow light leaking in from somewhere was just enough for her to see the pit in the tunnel floor, on the other side of the grill. A similar grill on the other side of the pit showed her where the tunnel resumed.

If the two obstructions weren't bad enough, what was scurrying around in the pit certainly were.

It was full of rats!

She couldn't count how many of them th most
but the thought of crawling through them the utter
enough to make her give up on the ears to her eyes
loneliness and despair she felt br
as she lay there.

But Liz thought of th collar and pulled herself
together.

She had to think clearly.

Then she remembered the ball gag and section of
grill she had dragged along, and a frantic idea scrambled
into her head. Within a couple of minutes she had
fashioned a kind of ancient fly swatter.

Pulling at the wire mesh, the malnourished vermin
trying to bite at her fingers, she managed to prise up a
tiny section. Immediately the creatures surged towards
it but she quickly pushed her improvised swatter
through the gap, closing it after, and holding it from
her side of the mesh.

It must have been five sickening minutes of steady
slashing and lashing of each horror which tried to get
at her through the tiny hole in the grill before the last
of the starved creatures was stilled.

After catching her breath for a few more minutes and
steeling herself again, Liz finally wrenched the grill
up. Sweeping aside the litter of scrawny bodies with
the swat, Liz crawled through the pit without looking
too closely at the things that touched her naked flesh.
As she struggled with the mesh on the far side she heard

a scuffle behind her and felt a furry body on her.
Screaming, she lashed out, kicking the stunned rat away
and struggling even harder until she was able to wrench
the grill free and crawl once again into the relative safety
of the dark tunnel.

She stopped when she was at last lying full length on
her belly in the tunnel but then, with a rustle, that final
persistent rat squeezed through the flap after her and
she felt its snout sniffing along her thighs. Liz had
discarded her bloodied swatter, so she could only strike
out blindly with her fist until the thing stopped moving.
She kicked it away back into the pit.

Liz almost vomited with revulsion. What would it
have been like to try and cross that pit with no weapons
and the creatures still alive? She shuddered at the
thought of using just her bare hands to tear the hungry
creatures from her vulnerable flesh in the darkness, then
to continue along the tunnel with the avaricious
creatures scrabbling in pursuit.

Regaining some semblance of control, she wiped her
nose on her bare arm and crawled off again into the
darkness. After a short while her questing arms felt a
gap ahead and she thanked the stars above for her
caution in not blindly surging ahead without caution.
Her groping hands identified another sharp bend in the
tunnel that plunged straight downwards. She carefully
leaned over the edge and reached down, but couldn't
feel the bottom, although she could hear more running
water. She squirmed around and was just able to turn,

slide forward, and lower her legs blindly into the inky hole. She sat on the riveted lip, exploring down into the darkness with her feet. She couldn't see the water lapping below her but, when she lowered herself slightly so that just the edge of her buttocks remained on the sharp edge, she felt the cold water flow against her toes.

Liz knew she had no choice, so she slowly took her weight on her hands and inched down, bracing herself, gasping at the shock of the cold water as it rose slowly up to her ankles, her calves, her knees. She began to fear the water was too deep, but her arms were almost at the point were she wouldn't have the strength to haul herself back up.

Was she about to plunge to her death?

What should she do?

Her arms began to quiver under the strain. She wanted to raise herself, but it was too late; her arms could hold her no longer. With a shriek her hands slipped off the edge of the tunnel and she sank into the murky depths. But she cracked her knees on the bottom, and managed to regain her balance and struggle up to the surface. The water came up to her breasts, and she thankfully gulped in air, coughing and spluttering and shivering.

Once she'd whispered a silent thank you, she explored with her feet. There appeared to be another bend in the tunnel – so that it proceeded horizontally again – beneath the surface of the water. She supposed it would have provided a suitable trap to prevent the rodents getting out of the tunnel had she not overcome the

With teeth chattering, she pragmatically identified her immediate problems. First, the fear of having to crawl into the unknown watery tunnel. Second, the time relentlessly ticking away.

There was absolutely no choice for her.

Taking a deep breath she ducked beneath the flowing surface and felt around with her feet and hands, but it became obvious that the tunnel continued underwater for some way, so she would have to turn back around and plunge head-first into it rather than feet-first.

Gasping with the physical effort, she managed to haul herself back up onto the lip of the tunnel and turn. Taking a deep breath she relaxed her shoulders and plunged head-first under the cold inky water. She nearly lost her nerve when her shoulders momentarily stuck on the sharp underwater bend, but then she was round it and frantically pulling and squeezing herself along under the water. Panic began to gnaw at the edges of her consciousness as the tunnel seemed to stretch on endlessly. Her lungs soon felt that they would burst. Once again she was filled with the dread of it all ending there, trapped naked and alone in the water-filled subterranean tunnel.

At last, though, her desperately clawing fingers felt another upward bend. She twisted round it with the last of her energy until she could straighten and thrust her head once again into the life-giving air.

The dark-haired beauty sat trembling with cold and

shock, rivulets of water coursing from her shivering body, up to her stomach in the icy water. Sucking in air, she took time to collect her wits and her breath after the ordeal. It was several minutes before she could again think clearly. She had lost all track of time.

The luxury of further thought was banished as her imagination transformed the band around her throat into a choking fist. Galvanising her protesting muscles into action again she wedged herself upward to haul herself, once again, into a dry horizontal tunnel.

After edging her way along Liz realised, thankfully, that the tunnel was becoming warmer. Indeed, warm air was blasting out of vents all around her. The metal that encased her soon became almost too hot to touch, and the shivering gave way to perspiration that stung her eyes. She slumped for a moment; hadn't they done enough to her?

Determined that they wouldn't beat her, she crawled on. Using knees and elbows, she tried to make only minimal contact with the hot metal, especially avoiding the sensitive skin of her breasts, face and thighs.

To reduce its contact, Liz was going much faster through the darkness, moving each limb to fractionally kiss the metal, taking her weight before moving it on. Thankfully her progress was made easier as the tunnel became wider and it was sloping down slightly. But suddenly and without warning she must have passed over a hidden pivot, because the entire length of pipe in which she was crawling suddenly tilted down. It was now too wide for her to brace herself and, screaming, she slid headfirst down the inclined tube to crash onto a pile of sacks in an ungainly heap of sprawling limbs.

She lay for a while, trying to make some sort of sense of it all. Perhaps the ordeal was over. At least she was out of those terrible tunnels. However, the sight of the other occupant of the room in which she had landed cruelly doused her initial relief.

Kate Crisp sat naked in a chair. Her wrists were strapped to each of its arms, her neck to the back and her ankles to each front chair leg. She couldn't talk because her teeth were clenched tightly around a large phallic-shape attached by a spring to a kind of pulley set on the floor right before her. Another phallic object, far from static, was positioned on a vibrator below a hole in the chair and was rigorously pumping in and out of the girl's vulnerable womanhood.

The effect on Kate was obvious.

Her face was flushed, her body glistened with perspiration, and her hips moved slightly above the continual thrusting.

Liz instinctively rushed forward, unable to abandon her despite a first warning beep from the collar and a sign around Kate's neck:

Prisoner Undergoing Punishment – Do not Touch

Kate listlessly opened her eyes at the sound of Liz. They immediately opened wider in alarm as Liz reached for the phallus in her mouth. Liz realised her colleague was desperately trying to give her a message as she moaned around the despicable phallus. Her eyes darted between it and the pulley, and she shook her head as best she could.

Gently, Liz gripped the phallus and eased it from between Kate's lips, holding it tight, keeping the tension on the spring. After briefly stretching her aching jaws Kate, stimulated by the other phallus still pumping into her sex, whispered to Liz.

'Please leave me, commander. They've said it'll be all the worse if anyone helps me. You must leave me here.'

Liz didn't know what to do. The collar beeped again, urging her to think quickly.

'Commander,' Kate continued, whispering, obviously trying to concentrate despite the inanimate thrusts between her legs. 'I… I must tell you. I heard from one of the crew before we were separated, that they're going to make the captain disarm *Explorer's* self-destruct. They – they know it'll otherwise activate if they…' she tried desperately to concentrate over the relentless stimulation between her legs, '…if they try to use the ship or its weapons. They f-figure they can make him… and the others who know the disarm codes…' she licked her lips and closed her eyes, '…use them.'

'Oh no.' This was a development Liz had dreaded. Including herself and Harry, five crewmembers knew the codes. After face-scans had confirmed their identity, any three of them had to simultaneously punch in their own secret numbers to deactivate it before the ship could be powered up. However, she knew a way of overriding the codes while giving the outward impression that they had been disarmed. To do so, every one of the three code holders had to exactly halve their code numbers. The system would show it had been apparently disarmed but, in reality, the destruction would only be delayed – until anyone tried to use the ship's weapons. She and Harry were the only ones to know of that particular ruse; a recent and secret modification. Liz realised that she needed to get the message across to all other code-holders who might be instructed to deactivate. That was Rose Pierce, Kate and Joanne. Swiftly, Liz whispered the alternative codes to Kate and asked her to pass them on to any of the others she came into contact with.

Liz felt a pang of guilt; she wanted to help Kate but the slightly increasing rapidity of the beeping reminded her with gut-wrenching dread of her own mortality. She could do nothing for the girl. Kate nodded in understanding after Liz had hastily explained her predicament and dashed for the door.

Next to it, on a small table, Liz noticed the familiar red catsuit, folded neatly with a note on it instructing her to put it back on.

Liz did so hastily and looked back sympathetically before tentatively opening the door and slipping into another dimly lit corridor.

Not knowing which way to go, she made up her mind, went right, and padded along on bare feet. After a few minutes she reached a dead-end. She cursed with dismay and turned quickly in the opposite direction. The corridor seemed to go on and on. The collar beeped ever more urgently. Her breath was rasping in her throat and the ordeal was taking its toll; exhaustion was beginning to creep into her body. But despite the effort she quickened her pace, the beeping collar a constant reminder of how little time was left.

She rounded a corner and shrieked as she cannoned into the huge bulk of the pirate who had first called them for interrogation after their capture.

'P-please, where's Stern?' she gasped, pushing against the fat slob's chest as he tried to wrap his heavy arms around her.

'My name's Keane,' he said, ignoring her question.

'Please,' she tried again desperately, 'where's Stern? I need to see her straight away.'

Keane's eyes roamed over her trembling body, and his chins wobbled as he licked his fleshy lips. Seeing the hungry look in his eyes, Liz shrank back against the wall behind her.

'You need to see Stern?' He chuckled. 'Then you'll have to kiss me first, my little beauty. And ask nicely.'

Liz knew she had little time to waste on the disgusting lecher, and reasoning with him was clearly not an option. It was hopeless; she had to do what he wanted – and quickly. She swallowed and moved close to the creep, the tips of her rubber-clad breasts almost touching the fat barrel gut of her tormentor.

'Come on, my little beauty, squeeze your sweet self up against me,' he encouraged crudely. 'Kiss me nicely and I might help you.'

Cringing with revulsion, Liz gingerly pressed her softness against the horrible smelly slob. Suddenly his huge arms were around her, one great paw crawling down her back. It squeezed the cheeks of her bottom painfully, pulling her against the hardness spearing from his crotch. His other hand squeezed and mauled her sickeningly. It made her squirm with disgust, but tentatively, closing her eyes against the nightmare, she lifted her face and pressed her lips against those of Keane. They felt like two slugs, and then his tongue, equally repulsive, squirmed between them and into her mouth.

At last he pulled away from the slobbering invasion of her mouth, his foul breath panting across her beautiful upturned face. 'I have to take you to Stern now,' he whispered, his voice thick with excitement. 'I'm not allowed to indulge myself any further with you... for now.' Liz closed her eyes and cringed, knowing what was coming. 'But we will have some fun together,' he went on. 'You just wait and see if we don't.'

With that Keane belched and pushed her along the corridor. With the collar beeping persistently he knocked on one of the many doors they passed, opened it and pushed Liz inside.

She stumbled to a halt, and was so thankful to see

Stern. The woman was lounging on a richly upholstered sofa, a glass of wine in one hand. She was wearing only a dressing gown.

'So, you made it then,' were Stern's only words; no recognition or praise for coming through the terrifying ordeal successfully.

'Yes, the collar, please!' begged Liz.

'Well, we saw from the vids monitoring your progress that you ignored the sign and talked with your female crewmember. That is a punishable offence, you know.'

'I-I'm sorry, it was just that I thought she w-was in difficulty. I wanted to help. Oh, please take this collar off. I've done as you wanted.' Liz didn't want to beg, but such was the reaction to her ordeal and her terror of the collar that she scarcely cared what she said. She just wanted to be free of the appalling threat around her throat.

'Well, I think I must punish you first, and then we'll see,' said Stern calmly. 'Incidentally, you've forgotten the respectful form of address. Ask correctly to be punished, and then we'll attend to the other matter...' she chuckled cruelly, 'assuming there's still time before it activates.'

Liz could have screamed with helpless frustration. Her hands flew to the collar in an instinctive but futile attempt to be rid of it. Was it tightening? The beeps were nearly continuous now. Would she actually get any warning or would it be instant, snapping tight and depriving her of air while the grotesque woman looked on? 'M-ma'am, please punish me now,' she said weakly, her shoulders sagging in defeat.

'Very well, my dear, I will punish you. Take off the suit. I want you standing by the sofa with one foot up on it, your hands on your head. I'm going to give you four strikes on each inner thigh with my trusty cane.'

Liz's stomach churned with apprehension, but she couldn't protest without wasting time. The cane was her only available route to getting the collar off.

She quickly undressed again and moved to the sofa, placing her right foot up on the seat, stretching the tendons of her thigh, then clasping her hands obediently on her head.

Maddeningly slowly, Stern took careful aim with her slim cane, tapping once, then twice. Then she whipped it up against the silky underside of Liz's thigh, midway between her knee and the curve of her bottom.

'Aaaah…' Throwing her head back, breath hissed through Liz's clenched teeth. The pain was excruciating as it burned into her sensitive flesh. She very nearly wrenched her foot down, only a supreme effort of will keeping it in place, her fingers locked more firmly on her head. She blinked back tears of pain and desperation.

The willpower required to maintain that position increased in commensurate intensity to the pain as the strokes of the cane marched steadily closer, and then bit into, the most sensitive flesh of all, in the crease under her buttocks where her delicate petals hid.

'Very good, my pretty,' Stern cooed. 'And now the other leg, if you please. And stop that pathetic sniffling.' She felt intoxicated with power as she forced the delicious girl to change her exposed position. She viewed with indescribable pleasure the delights of her sex peeping from under her raised thigh and delightfully pert bottom. She really was quite a catch. The delicately heart-shaped face was somehow enhanced by the tears trickling down it. The long dark hair flowing down over her shoulders and the dip in her spine leading to the swell of her buttocks really were to be admired. Her posture, knuckles white with tension, thrust forward her breasts and teasingly erect nipples.

Deliberately taking her time, knowing the girl's desperation for the collar to be removed, Stern bent a little to closely examine the well-proportioned inner thigh that had already received the cane's kisses. Four red weals of torment crossed the velvety flesh. Her victim gasped anew as Stern ran a fingertip down one of the lines she had skilfully raised. She wondered whether the girl would have detected the slight tremor as it passed across her moist love lips.

Stern savoured the warm liquidity of her victim before getting a grip of herself and applying four more scolding lines to the underside Liz's other thigh.

'There, that wasn't so bad, now was it?' she whispered to the tearful girl.

'Please, m-ma'am, the c-collar,' begged Liz, trying to ignore the woman's dry lips brushing her own.

'One final thing,' whispered Stern, tasting the girl's salty tears as she loosened and parted her gown. 'I'm going to have you now, as a man would.' She produced a black rubber dildo from a pocket of the open gown. 'But I'll first extend the time delay on your collar,' she said, deftly programming the buttons below Liz's chin. Liz exhaled with relief when the beeping was silenced.

'I believe I can do anything as well as any man,' Stern explained to the bewildered girl. 'And that includes the sexual act.' Liz couldn't believe what she was hearing. The woman had to be mad. 'Have you ever had sex with another woman before?' Stern asked, with a bizarrely normal air.

'I… no, ma'am.'

'Good, I enjoy taking a new girl for the first time.' The woman smiled thinly and stroked Liz's cheek. 'And don't worry, I'll instruct you in what to do. But just remember, I like to be pleased. Otherwise I can become awfully forgetful, and I might just overlook the need to deactivate the collar.' She licked her lips hungrily as she gazed over Liz's beauty. 'Mmm,' she murmured pensively, 'I'm going to enjoy you. Now, undress me and fit the dildo.'

Liz removed her hands from her head, and in an act that would have been unthinkable only a few days before, she slid the gown off the woman's shoulders. The woman wore only a pair of thick white knickers. Her skin was dry, and her small breasts sagged. Ignoring the rising tide of nausea, Liz bent and slid the knickers down her thin legs, to reveal a wiry bush. She felt the woman's fingers on her shoulders, pulling her up and then moving to cup her breasts. Following whispered directions she strapped the obscene black dildo around her tormentor's narrow waist.

Stern's breath quickened as she positioned her beautiful captive on the bed. The wonderful flower-like offering of Liz's sex pouted between her splayed thighs. She knelt between Liz's sculptured legs and probed both delightfully vulnerable orifices with a stiff finger, feeling them contract and grip. Then she shuffled forward and covered the lush body beneath her.

Constantly aware of the collar's threat, Liz reluctantly moved in rhythm with the woman lying on her, knowing she had to please the old crone. She held her breath as she felt the rubber snout probe her sex, and then her back arched as Stern triumphantly sank her hips and the inert column filled and stretched her. The bed squeaked quietly as the woman moved rhythmically, embedding the large dildo ever deeper into her victim. Obediently Liz followed the orders hissed into her ear and wrapped her arms around the moving woman, holding her just as she would her lover… Harry. The thought squeezed bitter tears from her tightly closed eyes. The tears meandered down her cheeks and soaked into the bed cover.

Cold thin lips sought and pressed against hers, the tongue and stale breath invading her mouth. Two claw-like hands thrust under her buttocks, pulling and impaling her ever deeper onto the wicked dildo. It pumped in and out like a piston.

A frenzy of action signalled that the hateful woman was reaching her climax. She thrust and panted more and more aggressively. She ordered Liz to cup and squeeze her buttocks and pull her deeper. At last the woman tensed and stilled, every sinew straining, mouth gaping, before she collapsed with a shuddering sigh on Liz's perspiring body. Despite her revulsion, Liz felt a knot of disappointment deep in the pit of her stomach that she'd not been allowed to reach her own orgasm, which had been creeping up within her. She wanted the rigid rubber impaling her to the bed to start its tantalising movements again.

But she was wrenched back to her awful reality as the collar beeped again. The woman climbed off her, attached a leash to the collar, and lashed that to the bed. Then she bound Liz's wrists behind her back with a pair of leather cuffs. Thus, quite helpless, Liz had to endure being snuggled up in the bed next to her captor.

Stern was in a twilight world of bliss. Drifting in and out of sleep she pulled the exquisite creature closer, feeling the softness and warmth of the gorgeous body pressed against hers. Her fingers trailed lazily through the girl's dark tresses, entwining, feeling the silkiness as it brushed her creamy shoulders.

Liz shivered with revulsion as the woman's hands cradled and stroked her. It was as if they were lovers, rather than a cruel woman with her helpless victim.

She stifled a sob. The bony hands travelled over her face, her lips, and so intimately, sensuously, through her hair. She shivered again, as her body was pulled closer to her tormentor's, moulding into it.

Stern traced down over the delectable curves of Liz's back. Then stroked over the smooth cheeks of her perfect bottom. The flesh quivered delightfully as her fingers delved into the cool cleft to stroke over the soft down lining the plump silken flesh of her love lips. Moving over those petals, a finger came to rest against the puckered entrance to the girl's bottom.

The fingers were horribly active, probing and delving with complete possession and freedom. Liz could do nothing but endure the molestation.

Stern savoured the feel of the girl wriggling uncomfortably, and then added to her woe by pushing her face down to her dry breasts and quietly ordering her to please her again. The muffled plea about the collar made her nipple stiffen in the warm wet mouth that obediently smothered it. As she savoured the feel of the busy mouth, Stern decided it would be nice to put the girl's talents to good use between her legs – but after she had fully enjoyed this attention and dozed a while longer.

Later, lying amongst a tangle of sheets, Stern smiled wickedly as her fingers worked deep within Liz's syrupy vagina while her thumb expertly flicked the encouragingly engorged bud of her clitoris. The girl's hips were instinctively beginning to writhe under her experienced ministrations, and fragrant juices squelched between her fingers. Stern, too, was giving herself over to the delights of yet another orgasm as the tongue, which she knew to be so reluctant, probed tentatively into her sex. She felt the heat increasing around her fingers, felt her fingers being gripped within those succulent petals. Just as the bubble of pleasure exploded within her the girl shuddered too, threw her head back, and gave herself up to the climax so knowingly coaxed forth by Stern.

Liz relaxed into the bed, and felt the woman's fingers fiddling again with the collar, resetting the timer. As she sought a little respite in sleep, she knew it was going to be a long night.

Chapter Nine

Stern pressed a button, the door to her chamber whispered as it slid open, and then she lounged back on her pillows again. She eyed Liz, standing before her in the delectable black leather bra and miniskirt she'd given her, her wrists still secured behind her back, thrusting those mouth-watering breasts towards her. 'I'm bored of you...' she said dismissively, as though tired of a new toy, '...for now. But have no fear, my precious one, you shall spend more nights here with me.'

Liz shuddered, not even certain whether she was repulsed or excited by the prospect. The woman had somehow unearthed strange desires she would never have dared believe existed within her during their night together.

'But now you'd better hurry along,' Stern went on. 'You only have an hour or so left on the timer, and I'd hate to think of my future fun being thwarted by that collar.'

'But...' Liz couldn't believe what the woman was saying. 'Please, you said you'd take this thing off me!'

'Then that will teach you to believe everything you're told.' The woman chuckled evilly. 'Now, leave me and seek someone by the name of Sulin. She'll deactivate the collar.'

'But—'

'Leave! I want to be alone, and you need to find Sulin sooner rather than later. Go!'

Liz was speechless. She knew further pleading was pointless, and so she turned and fled the room. The door hissed shut behind her and she was alone in the empty corridors, the constant electrical hum all around her.

Which way? Her head jerked from left to right. Who was this Sulin person, and where would she find her? It was surely hopeless. Why was Stern doing this to her?

Knowing that standing around would do her no good she decided to go right, and set off along the dingy corridor, her pace hindered by the leather cuffs on her wrists.

A long time passed and she saw nobody. She paused for a moment to catch her breath, wondering how on earth she would find this Sulin person, when suddenly her desperate thoughts were interrupted.

'Hey you!' A pirate appeared ahead of her and advanced aggressively. 'Where are you going?'

'I – I need to find someone called Sulin as quickly as possible – *arghh*!' Liz's hurried explanation was violently curtailed as a heavy boot swung up into her stomach, wrenching the wind from her lungs and making her sag against the wall behind her.

'Why?' he snarled, with unnecessary belligerence.

'Who are you? All I see is a Federation scum on the loose.'

'Puh-please.' Liz struggled for breath, her head throbbing as she slumped against the metal wall, unable to use her hands to protect herself against another unprovoked assault. 'Please don't hit me... I need to find Suh-Sulin... sh-she has to deactivate this collar... my name's Elizabeth Hartley—'

'Shut it, scum,' he cursed. 'No one gets through here without my say so. Stand up straight against the wall.'

Liz managed to get a lungful of breath and straightened up a little, trying to shield her abused ribs. Why had the brute reacted so violently?

He stepped close, his beady eyes studying his stricken enemy. 'Now then,' he said, his voice quieter. 'You just stand nice and still and quiet while I do my job.'

'Please, I must get to—'

With unexpected speed the pirate pressed a finger against Liz's lips, silencing her.

'Shhhh...' the finger pressed a little. 'I said nice and still, *and* quiet. Don't make me angrier than I already am. I don't like finding Federation scum roaming unsupervised around my section. Got it?' The pressure of the finger increased, and Liz could do nothing but allow her lips to peel apart and for it to push into her mouth.

The pirate smirked, pulled the finger out, cupped her chin, and pushed her head back against the wall. 'Now, I have to search you,' he went on, his face mere centimetres from hers. 'For all I know you could have a nasty weapon concealed somewhere.'

Liz closed her eyes and cringed as his free hand started in her hair, slowly crawled down her face to her throat, checked around her neck beneath her hair, and then slipped further down to her left breast. It cupped and squeezed through the snugly fitting leather. The fingers of his other hand dug into her cheeks, forcing her mouth open.

'Mmm, that feels nice,' he said hoarsely, mauling her breast, and then moving to the other. A thumb found her nipple, and the traitorous bud stiffened under the stimulation. The pirate smirked again. 'And you love it, don't you?'

His weight pressed her against the wall, painfully trapping her pinioned arms. 'Please…' How could she make the bully understand that she had desperately little time.

'Shhhh… quiet, remember? Now, we'll just check down here.' The hand lowered over her tummy as he continued the charade of searching her, and his breathing grew heavier in his throat. 'My word, but you're a pretty catch,' he panted. 'Spread your legs a little,' and he encouraged her to obey with the toe of a boot, nudging her feet apart. His groping hand slid up one tensed thigh, inched up beneath the taut leather hem, and his rough palm cupped the feminine swell of her panties. It was warm to his coarse touch, and he grinned lecherously. 'My, my – you *do* love it.'

'Please,' Liz tried again as he lifted her chin a little more, straining the tendons in her neck, and nuzzled into her throat, his whiskered jowl abrasive against her flesh as he breathed deeply her femininity. 'Please, I have to find Sulin.'

But she knew he wasn't listening; the face burrowing into her neck and the stubby fingers that were stroking the gentle swell of her leather panties and pressing them between her moistening sex lips clearly told her so. She just had to try something else before it was too late.

'Listen,' she whispered as seductively as she could in the circumstances, 'if you help me – if you take me to Sulin, I'll be especially nice to you…'

The slobbering stopped. She had his attention. Now she had to see her hastily conceived and foully onerous plan through.

His lips brushed her earlobe as he spoke. 'What kind of "nice"?'

Despite his crushing weight she managed to grind a hip into the bulge so blatantly pressing into her side. She swallowed deeply and prayed for her courage not to fail her, as she said, 'Whatever kind you like. It's up to you.'

There was a long silence, save for the constant electrical humming. Had she made a serious misjudgement?

Suddenly the savage grabbed her upper-arm painfully and propelled her along the corridor. The sudden flurry of activity caught her unawares, and before she could protest or ask what he was doing a door hissed open.

'In here,' he snapped.

'But—!'

Rough hands pushed her into the small chamber, spun her round to face him and pressed down on her shoulders. 'Get on your knees.'

The power in the hands gave her little chance to do anything else. She knelt humbly and lowered her eyes as the pirate frantically loosened his trousers and let them drop down his sturdy legs. Strong fingers dug into her cheeks again and lifted her face, and there bobbed his erection, his male scent invading her nostrils.

'Use your mouth.' His voice was strained by the intensity of his need.

'You must promise…' she insisted impotently. 'If I do this you must take me to Sulin…'

'If?' he sneered gruffly. 'Now do as I say… use your mouth.'

Liz knew it was hopeless. She just had to do as he wanted and hope there was an ounce of decency in the pirate. Her full moist lips peeled slowly apart, and as he grunted his approval and the throbbing bulbous head approached, she closed her eyes in resignation. It touched her lips, prised them further apart, and then forged inside, ploughing along her tongue and filling her mouth until his wiry pubic hair cocooned her nose and her leather-encased breasts moulded against his hairy thighs. Fingers dug into her scalp and began to glide her back and forth.

'Fucking hell…' he groaned, lifting his head and staring blindly at the ceiling as he revelled in the sensations her warm wet mouth were lavishing upon him. 'Shit… I *can't*—!' His words strangled and died in his throat as the suction around his cock proved too much and he erupted and spent in her delectable mouth like he'd never spent before. His chest heaved as he inhaled deeply and pulled her perspiring face into his groin, rocking against it as his spending continued, but gradually subsided in intensity.

Clenching her fists behind her back, Liz swallowed desperately, fearing she'd choke if she didn't. Eventually it was over and the softening penis slipped from between her lips, but Liz could do nothing more than kneel quietly, her head bowed. Even the threat of the collar could no longer rouse her.

The door hissed and the pirate turned to the lovely female who entered.

'Sulin,' he said as he refastened his trousers. 'What do you want here?'

Chapter Ten

The infrared vid-image showed a terrified, sexily dressed young woman sitting in a tiny upright hover-seat suspended a metre or so above the floor. Various clamps held her limbs and body immovably in place, fists clenching in tension around the restraints on the seat's arms. With her thighs secured apart, the white V of her knickers was clearly visible under a short black leather skirt. Her breasts, straining against a tiny black sleeveless jumper that left her toned midriff bare, were obviously unfettered by any bra.

Strapped in the seat in total darkness, Liz tried to control the hammering of her heart. Fear dried her mouth; fear of the unknown. She recalled the beautiful oriental-looking Sulin explaining the nature of this latest test, while closely watching her charge dress in her own clothes, which she selected for her as being some of the most provocative. Liz had never liked the theme rides at the futuristic parks that were now so prevalent on Earth, but a hideous parody of one was now taking her into the lair of something called the Beast, deep within the bowels of the pirate complex.

'We use the Beast for *messy* jobs,' Sulin had eagerly amplified. 'He's quite mad, lacking most human inhibitions. He's seldom allowed out of the depths beneath this place, but in return for his assistance with awkward interrogations we satisfy his childlike fascination for theme-park rides. He loves them, and his victims arrive spectacularly on one we've had especially designed and built him.

'Now, you've about two hours before the collar activates – unless you can persuade him to use his code. On the other hand,' she sniggered ominously, 'you might find the garrotte preferential to being the centrepiece of his fantasies. Just pray he doesn't choose to release the seat's clamps or arrange for it to crash before he indulges himself with you – that would be an even worse experience than spending time in his clutches...'

Although now still only a short distance away from the brightly lit control room and Sulin, Liz was already in a different world. The hovering seat had followed its invisible beam through heavy doors that shut behind her with a portentous finality, to suspend her in a frightening black void. Her senses detected stagnant water and she could hear something large wallowing in water far below.

A bloodcurdling screech swooped out of the darkness and something fluttered roughly across her face. She screamed and jerked away to the extent permitted by the strap around her throat, only just managing to control her bladder.

Before she could even consider what sort of hideous monstrosity had touched her, the chair lurched forward in a spine-bending jolt and, without warning, dropped into the darkness. After the initial gut-wrenching free-fall the compression of braking and shooting forward prevented her lungs from properly venting the scream her brain demanded. A dim light came from somewhere and illuminated the fact that she was about to be flung headlong into the waiting clutches of a huge squid-like creature, but another violent change of direction left the tentacles impotently lashing her legs as she flew past.

She was wrenched to a stop and flung upside down, only the clamps preventing her from falling into the filthy water she saw and smelt just below her sweeping hair. As she saw a disturbance on the surface heading towards her the chair whisked upwards, the lunging jaws of some unknown horror just missing her.

Liz heard a high-pitched giggle echoing somewhere in the distance and the chair again dipped lower. She was still upended just above the water, and she searched frantically for any evidence of some avaricious predator stalking her. Now she understood Sulin's comment about praying the Beast didn't amuse himself by releasing the seat clamps. For the first time in a long time Liz did pray – prayed that the restraints holding her to the seat would not open and let her fall into the mind-numbing horror below.

'Pleeease…' Liz's screech was silenced as the chair suddenly righted itself and dragged her rapidly upward and then forward in a stomach-churning wrench, her hair streaming behind in a dark blur. Strobe flashes showed her hurtling towards rock faces before suddenly lurching to the left or right at the last moment, or plummeting to whatever lay far below her.

When she wasn't screaming in terror her teeth were clenched, fingernails digging into her palms, all muscles knotted. Occasionally her wide-open eyes caught glimpses of a cackling blob of white flesh; the perpetrator of her terrifying ride. The Beast looked intensely ugly. Thankfully the ride gradually eased to a bearable pace, and Liz was able to see the man more easily. Unshaven, with long matted hair, he was grossly overweight. Naked folds of fat rippled as he gibbered insanely, clearly relishing his fun as he punched buttons on a remote control cushioned on his immense lap.

The seat continued to slow, but Liz knew it was sliding her down towards the gruesome man salivating as he manoeuvred her closer. Then the seat jerked to a halt, a metre above and in front of where he sat cross-legged, ogling her – his latest toy.

He pressed a button on the panel and the clamps pinning her to the seat sprang open. She rubbed her sore wrists and thighs, and then obeyed his gruff order and climbed unsteadily down and stood quietly before him. He inspected her thoughtfully, a slug-like tongue emerging to lap across thick lips.

'Very nice,' he eventually murmured. 'Much nicer than the usual sad specimens they send down to me. So why have they condescended to deliver such a delicious morsel for once?'

Liz didn't know how to respond.

'Got a tongue in your head?' he asked impatiently.

Liz nodded.

'Well, answer me.'

'This…' she gingerly touched the grisly collar, and then flinched, as right at that second it beeped, starting its chilling countdown.

'You want me to deactivate it and take it off,' he answered for her.

She nodded.

'And why should I want to do that?'

Liz couldn't think of any reason why he should, and lowered her eyes hopelessly.

'Perhaps I should interrogate you for information – that's what I usually do.' His matter-of-fact tone gripped Liz's stomach like an icy fist. 'But why should I do them any favours?' he nodded vaguely in the direction of the pirate colony above. 'Sending you down to my little world is the first memorable thing they've ever done for me.'

The collar beeped again.

The slug-like tongue slithered across fat lips again.

'What would you suggest?' he continued, goading his prey.

His prey shook her head, still gazing – without seeing – down at the ground.

'Mm?' he leaned a little closer, the folds of fat at his waist deepening. 'I can't hear you.'

115

Liz looked at him. 'I don't know…' she whispered. 'I don't know what to suggest.'

He lifted the control panel from his lap in one huge paw and placed it on the ground beside him. Liz noticed he was wearing a large soiled loincloth.

'Well, why don't you come and sit here while we discuss it?' He leered and patted his obese thighs. 'Come on,' he urged, giving her an encouraging wink with one bulbous eye.

Liz hesitated, dreading getting closer to the freak, but the collar beeped and propelled her into a response as though she'd been physically shoved forward. Her toes bumped against his shin and, deciding to get whatever it was he wanted over with, she started to turn so she could sit on his lap as prompted.

'Ah, ah,' he stopped her, reaching up with surprising speed to hold her trim hips. 'As you are, my dear.' And the hands slowly drew her down, the leather of her skirt catching the dull light as it rucked up her toned thighs and settled around her hips. She wasn't sure how he wanted her, but all she could really do was plant her feet on either side of him, bend her knees, and allow the downward pull to guide her onto his lap, sitting on his crossed thighs, her feet shuffling to rest behind him. 'There,' he grinned. 'That's nice, don't you think?'

Liz knew it would be sensible to agree, and so she nodded, albeit uncertainly. She'd expected him to smell abominably, but it wasn't a problem.

'Well, well,' he murmured, true admiration reflected

116

in his expression, 'you really are a special beauty. This must be my lucky day.' His bulging eyes roamed all over her face, and then down to the collar. His huge hands inched up from the leather skirt and encircled her naked midriff, powerful thumbs digging into her tummy. The collar beeped again, the warning sounds already alarmingly close together.

'So this is the little toy you need my help with, is it?'

'I—' her mouth was parched, and the words caught in her throat. 'I wouldn't call it a toy. Please, deactivate it and take it off me—' It beeped again and the man looked amused at the way poor Liz flinched at the sound.

He closed his eyes for a second and his nostrils flared as his head rolled back a little and he inhaled deeply. 'I can smell your fear,' he whispered, his eyes still closed, and Liz's stomach churned as she felt something within the loincloth lurch and stiffen against her bottom. The immense hands massaged in small circles, and inched upward beneath the cropped jumper, until they slid to her front and engulfed her naked breasts. 'I like the smell of your fear,' he whispered hypnotically, and opened his eyes again to stare deeply into hers. As the collar beeped again, and then again, Liz saw his pupils dilate, and knew her vulnerability was arousing the ogre. And incredibly that inexplicable thrill first awoken by the abhorrent Stern was stirring again. Thumbs flicked her nipples, and despite the awfulness of her situation, Liz couldn't suppress a throaty sigh of pleasure.

117

'So,' he whispered in a monotone, 'you want me to take the collar off.'

Liz closed her eyes and wallowed in the sensations the massaging paws and thumb-tips were creating.

'And what do I get in return?'

She barely heard the increasingly rapid warning sounds, so inexplicably intense was her excitement becoming. She covered the mauling hands beneath her own, her jumper sandwiched between them, and lewdly ground her bottom down in silent answer to his question.

'Seems good to me,' he breathed. One shovel-like hand slipped out from its cosy nest between her soft breast and encouraging hand and squeezed beneath her buttocks. It lifted easily, and Liz curled her redundant hand around the back of his head, entwining her fingers into his lank hair to help her balance.

His other hand pulled out from beneath her jumper, and as she dreamily cupped and squeezed her deserted breast she felt him rummaging between her raised thighs. She looked down into the humid shadows and saw the loincloth being peeled open, and then a handsome erection sprang up into view. The hand beneath her bottom guided her easily over the waiting weapon, but despite the unbelievable pitch of her desire she still had enough wherewithal to know she needed to retain her last bargaining chip.

'Please, wait...' she sighed, and reached down to grasp and pump his waiting cock in her perspiring fist.

She was rewarded by a sharp intake of breath. 'The collar…' she coaxed.

It was beeping rapidly now, warning of only minutes before it would contract and crush. The man touched it, stroking almost reverently. 'Okay,' he croaked, his voice thick with emotion and need. 'Okay.'

Liz drew her feet in and supported her weight on them, her arms on his shoulders, and squatted over his spearing erection, its bulbous tip pulsing against the soaking gusset of her white panties and pressing the material just between her juicy lips. She stared deep into his eyes, a triumphant smile flitting across her lips. Despite the ugliness of the man, there had somehow developed an unspoken bond between them. For some inexplicable reason she responded to him, unlike any of those bastards she'd encountered since her capture. His fat lips spread into a slack smile, and she knew he felt the same attachment to her.

His strong fingers tapped lightly and the dreaded collar fell silent. Liz whispered her relief and gratitude, and took a few seconds to gather herself, relaxing in the knowledge that the threat of the collar was no more, her fist lazily pumping the stalk that rose up between her thighs.

'Are you ready?' she asked, actually wanting to keep her part of the bargain. He nodded almost imperceptibly, holding his breath. Liz released his gnarled, turgid column, pulled the sopping gusset of her panties aside, and sank down until her bottom was once again nestled in his lap and he was fully embedded inside her clutching depths.

'Ah, how sweet,' Stern sneered under her breath as she watched the unlikely pair coupling on the vid-screen in her chamber. Because of the writhing couple's location the picture quality was poor, but she could see enough, and her talon-like fingers absently edged beneath the waistband of her heavy underwear.

She regarded the collar around Liz's slender throat, glinting dully in the murky light. The prisoner could have no way of knowing it was never armed. They needed her and most of the others as bargaining chips against each other, and especially against Clark. At least, until *Explorer's* self-destruct was deactivated.

Stern chuckled; of course, the delicious prisoner now grinding deliriously on the lap of that fat moron must not know her danger was non-existent; that the collar was nothing more than an amusing plaything. No, she musn't know that – not for a while, at least; the dark-haired beauty had yet more devious tasks to undergo and endure.

Chapter Eleven

Feeling awkwardly self-conscious, Liz could never in a million years have imagined herself in an outfit such as she now wore. Black leather ankle boots, black fishnet stockings and a suspender belt. Tiny black thong panties cut high on her hips left the magnificent globes of her buttocks on show. And a black bra cupped and pushed her breasts up and out, forming her deep cleavage into an enticing shadow.

But most humiliating of all was the cap perched on her head, with *Explorer's* crest pinned onto it.

After the comparative luxury of a night in a small cell, with toilet and washing facilities and a surprisingly comfy single bed, she was ordered to put on the skimpy outfit for the next phase of her endurance and penance test. She'd been told she was featuring at a guest night at something called the *Pussy Club*.

All day the tarty pirate girls who worked at the club had shown her – albeit with little interest – in how she was to perform, and now the butterflies were churning in her stomach as she stood in her scanty outfit behind a curtain off stage watching how several of the gum-chewing girls performed for their gawping audience. She cringed at the raucous comments and attempted groping by the prominently female audience – some feminine and some not so feminine – as the bored-looking girls took turns to gyrate around the stage. It was made extremely clear to Liz that, although they would allow for inexperience, if she failed to make a serious effort to entertain she would simply be stripped, bound and thrown into the audience for them to take into the various booths around the club to do as they wanted with her. That would be in addition to her crew also being punished.

The music stopped abruptly and the bleached-blonde on stage picked up her discarded underwear and strutted off, aiming the odd contemptuous kick at any stray hand that reached up from the audience and tried to fondle a part of her.

The moment Liz had been dreading had arrived.

'And now, ladies,' announced the butch compère, 'it is our great pleasure to introduce at the *Pussy Club* amateur spot for the first time, a genuine former space commander of the Federation who wants to entertain you to make amends for our continual harassment by her oppressive nation!'

Liz heard screams, whistles and catcalls as a hand shoved her in the back and the bright beam of a spotlight picked her out as she stumbled onto the tiny stage.

Brassy music started. With the bright light in her eyes Liz could see nothing of her audience, only thick cigar and cigarette smoke hanging over the shadowy mass like low thunderclouds. But she could hear their crude shouts and laughter, and she could sense the intensity of their hunger for her.

She tried to dance, but nerves made her naturally graceful rhythm desert her at the critical moment, and she knew her movements were wooden. She tried to move erotically, but felt it just wasn't happening. However, judging by the increasing fervour transmitting to her from the audience she was definitely doing something right. She tried to smile, as instructed.

The drunken clamouring throng of randy lesbians was baying for the chance to get their hands on the beautiful Federation officer trying so hard to please them. Hands thrust up from the heaving darkness offering currency discs. Some tried to get onto the stage, but the stocky compère strutted back and forth kicking them with scant concern for any physical damage caused by her steel-capped boots. At the same time her experienced eye was noting the highest bids waving in the wafting layers of tobacco smoke.

At last the vibrant music faded, but the raucous baying merely intensified as the mob knew it was time for one of them to get their hands on the naïve perspiring beauty.

The butch compère grabbed Liz's hand, and Liz barely heard the gruff command to follow above the din of the rabble before she was wrenched off the stage. She was led down into the mass of sweating bodies. The compère took one last scan around the frantically waving hands, and then dragged Liz to a blonde, who sat smiling inscrutably at Liz between sips of a gaudy cocktail.

'She's yours for ten minutes,' the compère shouted to the blonde above the curses of disappointment from all around, took the offered currency disc, and plunged it deep into her jacket pocket.

The music started again. The compère made her way back to announce the next performer, and all eyes turned to the stage – Liz forgotten. All eyes, except for Liz's, the blonde who owned her for the next few minutes, and a fat woman sitting next to her.

The blonde patted her thighs, and Liz understood the unspoken order and sat on her lap. An arm slipped around her shoulders and she was kissed immediately, and a hand cupped her breasts through the bra, incredibly long fingernails grazing the silky upper slopes that swelled tantalisingly from the lacy black cups. A tongue snaked between her lips and possessed her mouth.

Despite her discomfort at being in such a seedy den of iniquity, Liz found the blonde's attentions simply too much to resist, and the rest of the room was suddenly forgotten, her attention focused solely on the experienced fingers and tongue that were gifting her immense pleasure.

The kiss ended and the blonde nuzzled into her ear. 'Come on then,' she whispered, as the hand left her breast and wormed its way between Liz's thighs, and those knowing fingers pressed against the black material stretched over her delicate mound, 'we only have a few minutes left. I want you to come – right here on my lap.'

Liz was still aware enough of her surroundings for the prospect of having to respond to such a debauched order in the midst of the rabid rabble to shock her immensely. 'I—' But her protest was snatched from her lips as the fingers pressed more determinedly, urged the damp thong between her sex lips, and easily found her pulsing clitoris. 'Oooooh…' She shuddered, and welcomed the renewed kiss on her limply pouting lips.

The fingers strummed exquisitely, and were soon joined by the blonde's thumb. Liz's pleasure quickly rose to a pitch, the noise and heat around her fading to the back of her spinning mind. Once again the kiss ended. Liz opened her eyes to see why, and focussed dreamily as the fingers continued their task. The fat woman was whispering something to the blonde, who looked pensively into Liz's eyes. Then she nodded and the fat woman snickered, her mouth opening to reveal just one tooth. A currency disc was passed between the two women, and then the fat woman scraped her chair a little closer, so Liz was almost wedged between the two of them.

So ardent were the rest of the crowd with what was happening on the stage, that nobody seemed aware or interested in what was happening in their midst.

As the blonde continued to coax Liz to the brink of an orgasm, the fat woman gripped one of Liz's wrists and pulled her limp arm towards her lewdly spread thighs. All the time she grinned broadly at the swooning girl. Liz watched her hand being drawn towards the shadows, as though it didn't belong to her. She was feeling too languid and too excited to object in any way. The fat woman pushed Liz's hand beneath her own indecently short skirt. It was humid and her knuckles touched something, but a sudden deft touch by the blonde drew her attention back to the epicentre of her pleasure and she inhaled sharply, her eyes fluttering shut. Her fingers were guided further towards the waistband of the fat woman's knickers, and something still nudged the back of her hand. The woman snickered more loudly, and as Liz dreamily opened her eyes the fat woman seemed to loom over her. Her fingers were forced inside the knickers, and the fat woman curled and held them around... around... something hard and stiff!

Liz's eyes snapped fully open. The fat woman threw her head back and laughed hysterically, and the blonde timed her stimulation to perfection and took Liz over the edge into a wonderful spiralling orgasm.

'That's it – time's up.' The compère was back, gazing down upon Liz with little evident interest.

Liz sprawled exhausted on the blonde's lap, her arm still disappearing beneath the giggling fat woman's skirt, her fingers still curled disbelievingly around the erection that hid there. Despite her revulsion she couldn't let go, even though the fat woman had stopped guiding her and was now pushing her luck with the compère by mauling Liz's vulnerable breasts with undisguised relish.

'I said time's up,' the compère repeated angrily, and pulled Liz up by the arm. The blonde recommenced sipping her cocktail with an air of confident indifference, but the fat woman stood too. As the compère turned to lead Liz away the fat woman managed to hiss in Liz's ear, 'I'll see you later, dearie. Rules or no rules, I reckon you'll be worth it…'

And then the compère was weaving through the throng, with a bewildered Liz stumbling in tow.

She was taken to a booth. It was simply a small carpeted cubicle, clearly for the private use of the club members. The furniture consisted only of a bare stripped bed, a side-table and a chair. To her utter surprise, Liz saw Rose Pierce sitting naked on the bed, knees drawn up to her chin to preserve some modicum of modesty.

'You two are going to perform together on the bed,' announced the compère. 'The 3D vid will relay it to the audience on screens, if they wish to watch. I think you both know what your fate will be if it's not good enough. You start in about five minutes when you hear the buzzer and the red light comes on.' She sniggered derisively. 'But it's not all bad – drink these.'

The masculine woman poured two large glasses of sparkling white wine.

'You'll each drink the whole glass. It'll help relax you and increase the likelihood of you performing with genuine gusto. My members don't like to be short-changed.' With that the door was locked and the two

127

girls were alone together.

Looking resignedly at each other they sipped some wine. Liz drew her knees up under her chin, like Rose had, in a hopeless attempt to shield her body and lurid outfit and introduce some normality into a bizarre situation. She shuddered as she thought about the fat hermaphrodite, but hastily put the memory behind her; nothing about this colonisation should surprise her any more, and she had far more important matters to deal with.

Although knowing the booth would be under visual and audio scrutiny, she knew their was now a chance of whispering the message given her by Kate about the pirates disarming *Explorer's* self-destruct system, and also her plan for halving the numbers to thwart them. Either she, Kate or Rose might then at some time be able to pass the message on to Joanne. Hopefully Harry would anticipate their game-plan and follow suit. Thus, whichever three crew the pirates picked to deactivate the mechanism, they would all use the alternative numbers. If all the codes weren't halved the destruct would immediately activate and it would be a suicide mission. But that was surely preferable to a continued existence on the living hell that was Magellan.

The two drained their glasses. Liz hadn't drunk alcohol for a little while, and neither had she been permitted much food, so she found herself becoming rather light-headed rather quickly. She suspected also that the drink had been laced with something to enhance, for the added enjoyment of the audience, her performance with Rose – who was admittedly lovely.

True to the compère's words, her musings were interrupted about five minutes later by the sound of a buzzer, and then the normal light changed to a soft red glow.

Liz looked apologetically at Rose, shrugging her shoulders as she set down her empty glass and then swung round to face her. Her breath quickened as she realised just how attractive she found the enticing curves of her lieutenant's exquisite nudity, sexily indistinct under the defused red light. Liz pressed her thighs tightly together and tried without success to repress a shudder of desire. Rose's eyes were sparkling green pools of desire, shielding unfathomable lagoons of beauty. Curly blonde hair danced suggestively around her doll-like face as she innocently tilted her head to one side.

Rose, too, was breathing heavily, her glistening lips slightly parted as she opened her arms in invitation, the movement making her breasts rise deliciously. Then, as she swivelled to sit up straight, her beautiful thighs parted to reveal the downy triangle protecting the intimate secrets of her waiting womanhood.

Both girls realised they were hungry for each other, and the reasons for it did not seem important to them at that moment. Liz could feel herself losing concentration and realised she had to pass on the message before she was consumed with the rapidly approaching waves of desire that threatened to envelope her.

Neither gave any further thought to the many eyes that were no doubt watching them on the 3D screens outside. Their limbs entwined and pressed together. Liz was rapidly losing control, so she urgently pressed her warm mouth over Rose's parted, sensuous lips, tasting her sweet breath as their tongues entwined. She broke away to kiss the beautiful pulsing throat, moving round to a shell-like ear. She urgently whispered, imparting the message about the deactivation code. At the same time, for the benefit of the watching cameras, she gently nibbled and licked the delicious ear. Although Rose was writhing beneath her, she had the wherewithal to gently squeeze Liz's hand to confirm she understood everything – before both girls lost themselves to matters of the flesh.

Two pairs of erect nipples danced sensuously together as their kissing became more and more urgent. Their bodies locked together in a dance of passion, thighs pressed between moistened thighs. Liz gazed down upon Rose's graceful lines, worshipping her breasts with her hands. Then they rolled and their positions reversed. She eagerly took the rubbery tips of the blonde's breasts deep within her mouth as they hovered above her, sucking and nipping them alternately, drawing little whimpers from her lover. Looking over a smooth shoulder she shivered in delight at the sight of the sleek curve of the girl's spine, dipping before swelling into the perfect spheres of her buttocks –

clenching with desire.

Their fingers were probing the hidden delights between each other's thighs. Liz ground her palm urgently against the hard bud of Rose's desire, feeling the warm wetness there, then pushing a finger deep within her velvety depths. The blonde squirmed around, her inner muscles contracting to hold the plunging digit. Similarly a finger wormed inside Liz's soaking thong and thrust deep into her, and it became the centre of her universe, the giver of exquisite pleasure.

'Kiss me,' breathed Rose, and Liz understood the simple request.

She turned so her face was against the writhing warmth of the blonde pubis, drinking in the feminine smell, the delicate hairs tickling her nose and lips. She grasped the firm cheeks of Rose's bottom, her tongue trailing over a fluttering inner thigh to her love lips. With an exquisite pang of desire she then felt Rose's tongue thrusting into her own eager liquidity, the fingers holding aside the material to allow access. A glowing bubble of desire was building up within Liz, and she knew her colleague was savouring similar sensations. They writhed together, the sheen of their mutual desire glimmering on their flesh under the soft light.

While her tongue delved and probed in Rose's honey pot, Liz pressed a finger between her buttocks, against the secret opening there. She pressed again, and a little whimper from the blonde accompanied her finger as it sank just inside, met a little more instinctive resistance, and then sank further into her most private passage. With breathless anticipation she felt Rose reciprocating, fumbling with adorable inexperience between her buttocks too. Liz nibbled her lower lip as she waited – suspended – and then her back arched as an inquisitive finger prodded, nudged, and then entered her bottom. She momentarily withdrew her lips from the succulent flesh, her neck straining back, her mouth open as Rose's tongue and finger darted ever deeper in unison. Liz gazed wistfully at the glistening love juices clinging to the delicate blonde down covering her friend's pouting womanhood. Once again she buried her face into the girl's trembling femininity, feeling her vagina welcome her avid tongue. She felt the blonde's hips jerk and shudder in the throes of an orgasm. Then she herself reached the point of no return, no longer able to hold back. That desire erupted as she cried out with pleasure, convulsing helplessly under Rose's active tongue.

Although another act had started on the stage, the raucous audience at the tables was applauding ecstatically as they watched on the screens the heavenly bodies entwined on the bed and bathed in a red glow in the little booth. They were enjoying it all the more because the two sexy beauties were officers from the hated Federation.

As the two wallowed in the aftermath of their pleasure, the screens flickered off and there was a groan of disappointment from the gawping mass of sweating women.

Two of the mass rose quietly, unnoticed by the rest; a majestic blonde and her grinning, bulky partner in crime.

Chapter Twelve

In total contrast to the perverted big city sleaze of the *Pussy Club* was the neanderthal squalor of the shanty town alongside the Magellan spaceport. To Liz it seemed that civilisation had ended when she left the moving public walkway. Not surprisingly, it was the only auto-walk route that led in that particular direction.

She had at least been grateful for having some time in the comparative ease of her cell, instead of being interrogated further or used as a means to satisfy some pervert's lurid fantasies. The image of the blonde and the gross hermaphrodite slipping into the booth and locking the door permeated her mind, but she quickly banished it.

Since then she had still been in isolation from the other crewmembers, but just hoped that either Kate or Rose would have the opportunity to bring Joanne into the scheme of the self-destruct codes.

As it was practically dawn before she was taken from the club, she'd been left until past midday to sleep the debauched excesses of the place off. Her grudging gratitude, however, had vanished with the realisation of what her next ordeal involved. But having struggled through everything so far, and knowing what was at stake, she had a grim determination to conquer whatever perversities they could dream up – no matter how awful.

Liz had found herself on the near deserted walkway in a totally repugnant world of the troll-like dwarfs. She reached the end of the auto-walk and gazed around with trepidation. Apparently Mungo lived with his mate in one of the countless wooden huts dotted around. As she gazed anxiously at her strange new surroundings she was beginning to collect an inquisitive audience of dirty looking dwarfs. Her slender beauty stood out easily a good half metre above most of them. The Federation captive was a curiosity; no doubt the local vid-news had announced her humiliating servitude to Mungo.

However, there were other aspects besides her seductive shape and size that made Liz's arrival in the squalid town somewhat of an event. For instance, she was naked but for a leather harness. The straps of it did nothing to conceal the magnificent thrust of her bosom, the globes of her buttocks and her shapely legs. Her majestic form was in stark contrast to the squat bodies that curiously surrounded her. Furthermore, Liz had her arms outstretched across a heavy wooden yoke fitted across her shoulders, and onto the ends of which her wrists were tightly strapped. Mungo had also insisted, when collecting her that afternoon, that she be gagged with a leather bridle type affair.

'I don't want no fancy back-talk from her,' was his subtle way of expressing the request to Stern. Thus, Liz was unable to offer any objection to her treatment.

Probably, however, the most unusual aspects of all were Liz's method of arrival and the control being exerted over her. She was harnessed into the shafts of a cart, upon the seat of which Mungo sat, directing her with a set of reins attached to the bridle.

As the hunched natives shuffled closer Liz wondered what she was supposed to do next, but then a stinging pain flicked across her back, making her wince and reminding her of just how degrading her predicament was. The sharp flick was his command for her to begin pulling the cart now the aid of the auto-walk was no more. The reins tugged on the right corner of her mouth, telling her to head in that direction.

The whip struck again. Liz's breath hissed through teeth clenched tightly on the bit in her mouth. But she took up the burden of the cart and walked along the well-trodden path like an obedient pet, trying to ignore the vile comments and surreptitious mauling from the curious onlookers. She shuddered; she hated the dwarfs. She hated their diminutive and misshapen forms, and their touch made her skin crawl just as the close proximity of a hairy spider did – and now she was amongst them in their world, helpless and vulnerable. Clearly the pirates understood there was little that could be more distasteful for someone of her status.

The whip cut down again, viciously wrenching her thoughts back to the present.

'Move faster,' Mungo ordered brusquely, clearly enjoying his moment of glory. 'I want to get home sooner rather than later.'

Liz broke into a trot, ignoring the whoops and jeers of the dwarfs who scampered alongside, just like the sightseers who flocked around *Explorer* in their private spacecraft whenever the awesome ship arrived home victorious from a bloody campaign. She pulled her hideous burden on the creaking cart, hoping she wouldn't receive another painful slash from the whip.

Unfortunately for Liz there were several turns along their route. She was bathed in a patina of sweat, flared nostrils gasping for breath, as she trotted along frantically trying to anticipate the direction she should take to prevent the bit from being tugged too hard in her mouth.

Compounding her humiliation and discomfort was the ache in her shoulders and back, and her general fatigue in having to pull the weight of cart and rider. So she was desperately thankful when at last Mungo shouted for her to stop, even though he also emphasised the order by sadistically jerking on the reins.

Liz bent slightly from the waist, filling her lungs deeply and trying to ease her breathing. The reins slackened and the shafts dipped and rose as Mungo climbed down from the cart. A new voice spoke, and Liz looked up at a female dwarf. Grinning proudly, Mungo put his arm around her shoulder and introduced Greselda – his mate.

Peering at the odd couple through a damp fringe, Liz saw behind them their abode. It was a small hut with a smaller sloping-roofed lean-to adjoining one side, set in a roughly cultivated garden.

She shivered as the toothless female shuffled over. Wizened hands began inspecting her as though she was prize animal stock. The hateful touch made her shudder. She could do nothing but stand docilely while the examination took place. The hands lifted her long hair, fingers probed her ears. Then, even worse, making Liz snort through the bridle, the rough hands of the tiny hag groped the sensitive flesh of her breasts, squeezing and pinching.

Greselda pronounced herself satisfied after patting Liz's thighs and cupping, then slapping, each cheek of her firm bare bottom.

'Aye, she'll do I guess. No fat, but quite firm and strong. Good for breeding, if we keep her.' The dwarf's chest wheezed unhealthily as she cackled, her shoulders jerking up and down in a way that would have amused Liz in more favourable circumstances. As it was she froze with dread at the thought of being a permanent slave to the grotesque little people.

Later, while the weird couple ate a succulent-smelling evening meal of roast meat, Liz had to kneel on the rough wooden floor by their table, still burdened by the heavy yoke, although thankfully the bridle had been removed. Without the bit in place she was able to flex her jaw, and the relief was wonderful.

Despite her ordeal, the odour of the sizzling meat intensified her hunger, but there was no indication that she was to be fed. Mungo would give menacing little flicks of his whip if she even gave the slightest movement to relieve her aching back from its erect posture.

Finally the couple had finished. They pushed back their plates of remaining uneaten food, wiped their greasy mouths and chins on their grubby sleeves, and belched sickeningly.

'Come here, girl,' snapped Greselda, as Mungo made Liz crawl round to his mate, who threw her small lumps of meat.

The shame of being abused in such a demeaning manner burnt deep into Liz's soul. She was being treated like an animal by members of a race who wouldn't be allowed to remain in the same room as her without permission back on Earth. But the ever-present threat of the whip gave her no choice, and she couldn't fight back while bound to the yoke.

And she was starving.

It was difficult for her to eat properly off the grimy floor, and congealing grease coated her chin. But the meat was admittedly delicious and the warmth of it in her belly was some small comfort. When the last scrap had been devoured she was then given some surprisingly pleasant juice to drink, and began to feel a little better, her spirits rising a fraction.

Before the three green moons of Magellan signalled dusk, Mungo attached two heavy buckets to each end of the cruel yoke. Thus, festooned like a pack animal, she had to make several trips to a nearby well, wait while Mungo drew water, and then carry the slopping liquid back to top up their supply pit. If she spilled any he would curse and slap whichever of her thighs was within reach, making her yelp as much from the indignity of being treated like an errant child as from the actual pain of the stinging cuff.

After darkness had fallen she was shoved into the inviting lamplight of the hut. There was a metal tub already filled with water.

'You smell,' Mungo said brusquely, clearly making the most of being the boss around the place as he removed the yoke. 'We'll wash you.'

Liz's spirits rose yet a little more as the warm and pleasantly fragrant water soothed her aching muscles, and surprisingly skilful hands soaped and relaxed her.

All too soon the enjoyable bath was over; so soothing had it been that Liz was able to ignore the fingers that took surreptitious liberties with her beneath the soapy water.

Greselda then dried her and Mungo took her to an internal wooden door leading to the lean-to. The small area was filled with straw and Liz was unceremoniously shoved in, ducking sharply so as not to bang her head on the frame, and the rickety door was slammed and bolted from the outside. The lean-to was quite small and smelly, with no windows. The loneliness of solitude quickly crushed the veneer of her slightly increased spirits, and she curled into a ball in the straw, sobbing quietly, sleep alluding her weary mind and body.

But at least she was warm and fed, and for that small mercy she was grateful.

Time drifted, but then a sound made her quickly snap her eyes open and she squinted against the shaft of light that picked her shape out in the straw. Although the light was fairly subdued, its sudden invasion into the surrounding darkness to which she'd become accustomed made her shield her eyes against it with one forearm. Peering warily into the dull glow, she could make out the squat silhouettes of the two dwarfs standing in the doorway. They whispered to each other, too quietly for Liz to make out what they were saying, and then moved into the room.

'Wha... what do you want?' Liz managed to ask, lifting herself onto one elbow so she half sat half lay, and watching as the shadow of Greselda collected a bucket from one corner, moved closer, turned it upside down, and then sat on it. The little female beckoned with a finger. With a sinking heart Liz, knowing she had no choice but to obey, and hoping they weren't intending to do what she suspected, got up onto her knees and shuffled closer.

There was a strange atmosphere in the tiny room, and no further words were spoken. Greselda took Liz's hands in her own, moved her thighs slightly apart, and pulled the beautiful girl even closer. She then cupped the back of Liz's head, eased her forward and down onto her lap, and rhythmically stroked her long silky hair with one hand and the uppermost side of her face with the other, as though she was a favourite pet. Almost imperceptibly, the female dwarf started to rock gently back and forth in unison with her stroking fingers.

When Liz heard Mungo shuffling behind her she knew exactly what was coming, but didn't react in any way whatsoever. Partly because the undeniably soothing touch of his mate was lulling her into a state of deep relaxation, and partly because she knew any resistance was pointless.

Clammy hands gripped her hips tightly. She did reach back – albeit without real conviction – but the fingers moved from her face and hair, caught her wrists, pulled them back behind the hips of the sitting female dwarf, and one hand crossed and held them there together. Then the calming fingers returned to her hair.

Apart from fairly heavy breathing from the kneeling and highly aroused Mungo, the eerie hush still cloaked the three shadowy occupants of the lean-to, and the weak light filtering through the slightly open door from the other room gave Liz the surreal feeling that she was dreaming.

Then she felt the very obvious pressing of an erect penis between her thighs, and knew that she wasn't.

The grip on her hips eased her back a little, the fingers stopped moving in her hair, the bulbous helmet nudged between her moist sex lips, and then her mouth slowly opened in a silent groan as the dwarf's girth and length stretched and filled her.

His humid groin pressed against her bottom and Greselda, with a faint grunt of approval, started stroking the kneeling girl's head again. Liz quivered all over, feeling totally impaled on Mungo's cock. He began moving steadily, ploughing back and forth. Liz whimpered, loving the sensations he was awakening and appalled at her own shocking weakness. As he rutted she was shunted against the sitting dwarf, her head rocking against the cushion of a soft belly and thighs.

Despite feeling ashamed by her simple submission to the pair, Liz knew her orgasm was upon her and she could do nothing to resist it. As Mungo stabbed with his hips more aggressively than before and stiffened, groaning throatily in the inky shadows and spitting his seed into her depths, she sighed with him and convulsed meekly on the lap of the female dwarf who was restraining and stroking her.

After a long night of little sleep Liz had to kneel again at the table and be fed scraps for breakfast. Greselda then took her outside, the neighbouring dwarfs laughing, as she was pulled along on a lead to be hosed down. She squealed and ducked and cowered as the cold water sprayed all over her body, her arms raised in a futile attempt to shield herself from the shocking dousing that wrenched the air from her lungs. Greselda especially directed the nozzle between her legs, much to the added amusement of the watchers.

Liz toiled all day under the hot suns, working in the fields under the direction of Mungo's whip, trying to ignore the dwarfs that still gathered to see the Federation enemy at first hand.

At the end of a long day she was hot and tired, dripping perspiration, her matted hair plastered to her forehead, cheeks, neck and shoulders. Every aching muscle yearned for some rest. It was with immense relief then, that she was washed again – this time enjoying the refreshing sluicing-down – and fed, and then harnessed back into the cart to pull Mungo back to the auto-walk, and back to the pirate's sector.

While the two dwarf's said goodbye to each other, Liz waited between the shafts of the cart and chuckled – quietly but almost hysterically; unbelievably, she was actually feeling relieved to be going back to the pirates!

Chapter Thirteen

Liz was positioned in exactly the pose demanded by the vid-man, who was making a film of each prisoner. Having been given scant time to compose themselves and without being able to confer, they had all been individually taken to the room by guards to make a plea for mercy. Liz was told, as were the others, that any refusal to comply would swiftly result in her execution and retribution against the rest of the crew. In addition to being sent to the Federation government and media, a copy of the vid would also be sent to their families to increase the pressure on Earth to make a deal.

With her back proudly erect and chin held defiantly high, Liz began reading the text she'd been given.

'People of the Federation, since our capture by the conquering and just forces of Magellan, I have come to realise the gross folly of our government's continued venture in this region. Here, we are the dictatorial rebels terrorising a passive and caring community that wishes for nothing more than to be left alone in peace. I am deeply ashamed of the Federation's belligerent attitudes and actions, which have left so many innocent men, women, and children dead or injured or orphaned. It is time we left these good people alone, otherwise we cannot complain or blame them if we suffer severe reprisals. Any retaliatory actions they are forced to take would be justifiable measures of defence, whereas our actions, past present and future, are nothing less then provocative aggression.'

The vid-man stopped filming and switched off his camera. 'That's it,' he said to his assistant, chuckling as he worked. 'That'll be a good one, coming from the second-in-command of their prized warship.

Chapter Fourteen

The following day the crew was fallen-in to rigid ranks – the authority of the officers further undermined by being placed amongst the ratings – and told they were being taken to several different prison camps. The reason given was in case the Federation foolishly considered a rescue.

Liz knew, however, that rescue was basically an impossibility. The Federation, even with spy satellites and probes, wouldn't know the exact whereabouts of the prisoners, and even if they did the fastest of their vessels would be detected so far out in space as to allow the pirates days to relocate and hide the crew again.

Or kill them.

And she also knew the Federation would never negotiate with the pirates.

No, they were alone, and if they were ever to escape they would have to do it alone.

It was a sweltering day and the twenty or so male and female crewmembers in Liz's group had been force-marched for many hours through sparse countryside. Initially they had been taken, bound and gagged, from the space centre in a covered hover-wagon. When they'd been loaded into the vehicle Stern had been there, an amused look on her face.

'Just a little warning, my dear,' she'd hissed, grabbing Liz's tunic and yanking her close. 'Your crew is being split up and this party, with you in it, is going to a detention centre. Forget your rank, you'll be just another scum prisoner, your only duty to obey orders. If you cause trouble or try to organise your crew in any way, you'll be in serious trouble and so will your people.' She stroked Liz's face with an icy hand and licked her lips voraciously. 'I'm sure a pretty thing like you will be warmly received where you're going.' She smiled cruelly, running her bony fingers down to pat the taut buttocks beneath Liz's thin prison uniform. 'Just be an obedient girl and work hard, and you may just survive the regime awaiting your arrival.' She kissed Liz lightly on the lips. 'And then you can come back to me and we'll continue where we left off. Now won't that be nice?'

Liz had nodded, knowing it was the only response that would be tolerated.

When they were eventually turned out of the vehicle they had absolutely no idea of their whereabouts or in what direction they were heading.

To further demoralise they were shackled together in three lines of six or seven. They were secured at metre intervals by lengths of heavy chain that was attached to metal collars around their necks, and their hands were bound behind their backs. A dispirited rabble, their bare feet soon became sore as they shuffled over the rough ground, wearing only their striped uniforms.

Liz knew this was a critical period in their incarceration; many of her crew were close to breaking, and if they were to have any chance of ever getting away from Magellan she would have to search deep for any reserves of her leadership qualities.

The pirate guards had given no recognition to her rank, making it even harder for her to lead her demoralised people. She moved along in the middle of a row, her body drenched with sweat. But the biggest thing praying on her mind was that neither Harry nor Joanne was amongst the group. They were the last remaining parties to the self-destruct codes and with whom she had been unable to make personal contact.

At last, hobbling around an outcrop of bleak sun-scorched rocks, they saw a formidable stockade across the shimmering heat of the baron landscape. It looked to be about a kilometre or so in the distance.

As they at last approached they heard the electric crackle of hidden defences being deactivated. As the tall gates creaked slowly open like a huge mouth wanting to devour the Federation traitors, the guards, showing off for the camp authorities, urged their exhausted prisoners to trot into captivity.

Gasping with the exertion, Liz saw the afternoon sun glinting on rolls of barbed wire, and the infrared beams and searchlights which surrounded the many sturdy brick and wooden buildings in the compound.

Within the high walls there were many other prisoners. They were mostly in all male or all female groups, toiling under the barked directions of vicious guards of both sexes, including some dwarfs. The prisoners were manually digging or carrying heavy rocks and timbers.

The huge double gates swung shut with a thunderous boom, the finality of the fearsome sound making Liz and her party flinch as an almost tangible cloak of dread enveloped them. But they weren't able to dwell on their miserable predicament, for with chests heaving they were lined up before a whitewashed brick building.

When the frightful neck shackles were removed, Liz and the others had the luxury of stretching tired limbs and regaining their breath. Then they all had to stand stiffly to attention under the sun while the pirate guards lounged in the shade, sipping iced drinks. The new prisoners longed to rest or find a cool respite from the merciless late afternoon sun. Yet they knew that with Magellan's thirty-hour day and tropical temperatures for so much of the four hundred day year, such a relief was unlikely. This would be another weapon used against them by their captors.

At last, after an hour or more, their arrival was acknowledged. An older man in an ill-fitting black uniform strutted out to inspect them. Liz eyed him cautiously, and comparisons with a toad came readily to mind. He was shaded from the sun's cruel rays by a submissive looking girl, who held a parasol over his head. She looked young, the wide-eyed innocence of her face framed by long fair hair. Her lithe body moved gracefully beneath a long white gown. The gown was belted tightly at the waist and split up one side, and as she walked it displayed tantalising glimpses of a slender thigh and calf. Pert breasts, clearly unfettered, moved enticingly within their translucent white confines. With downcast eyes the shame of her subservience was evident.

Liz wondered who she was.

A tall austere woman also accompanied the man. She too wore a black uniform, but hers fitted perfectly and clung to her voluptuous curves as she walked with hips swaying. Her dark hair was pulled back into a severe bun, and her scowling oriental eyes scanned the unruly ranks of prisoners with effortless sweeps and evident contempt.

Finally came another male. His sinister stare made Liz shudder when it swept over her. It was, she realised, the arrogant look of a man who knew he had total control over his hapless victims and despised their weaknesses. He would have no scruples or conscience to care any more about a fellow human being than he would an ant.

The three menacing figures carried short riding crops with flails. Gruff orders from the guards made the prisoners stand even more stiffly to attention as the three walked down their ranks.

'My name is Stefan Rolf,' announced the toady man, once the charade of the inspection had been completed and he stood at the front of his prisoners, beneath the

151

shade of the parasol. 'I am in charge here.' He indicated the tall woman next to him. 'This is my number two, Koolin. Some of you may recall her sister from the space centre, Sulin.'

Without taking his eyes from the exhausted ranks, he indicated the other man. 'This is Stone. He's relatively new here, but extremely eager to learn.' A thin smile lifted the corners of his mouth. 'And believe me, he's learning from an expert tutor.'

The toady man started to strut slowly to the right, almost catching the lovely girl with the parasol off guard, and she had to be alert to prevent any of the setting sun from touching his ruddy face.

'Welcome to Detention Camp Six,' he continued, as though not noticing the girl's lack of concentration, although Liz just knew it had been noted and filed away for future reference. 'There is only one rule here; you obey all orders instantly and without question. Myself, Koolin and Stone are your only gods. You will listen to no one but us. If any of the guards give you an order you can rest assured it has come from one of us, and so you will obey. If we say it, you do it – immediately.

You will work hard here building leisure facilities for me, my staff, and the guards; it is always necessary to supplement the standard accommodation for their comfort. You will also learn about our Magellan empire; it will correct the propaganda you have previously been indoctrinated with by your government and your military leaders.'

A shudder of pleasure rippled through Rolf. He loved the moment when new prisoners made their first acquaintance with his camp, loved the sheer power he had over them, and loved their despair as they realised that fact. They were now his and he had power of life and death over them. Not that this was totally true with the ragged batch before him. They were Federation crew and the authorities wanted them more or less intact for political reasons; a bargaining chip, he surmised. Still, he reasoned, the prisoners themselves would not know that, and some of them definitely had potential.

His eyes particularly lingered on the woman he recognised from the documentation and wanted posters as Elizabeth Hartley. He would certainly enjoy having such a beauty staying at his pleasure. He knew that back on Earth she was something of a celebrity; a courageous beauty with intelligence and breeding to match. At that moment, however, she was just a fearful young woman standing inconspicuously in a baggy and dusty prisoner uniform. But despite the grime her splendour still shone through, and he tried to visualise her toned body within the drab clothing. Another shiver of expectation rippled his jowls – he wouldn't have to merely imagine for too much longer!

And there were other pretty ones too. Not in the same league as Hartley, but pretty nonetheless. And some of the male prisoners were more than agreeable. Particularly the younger ones. Yes, thought Rolf, he would certainly have fun with this latest consignment of inmates.

A sliver of sunlight briefly cut across his face and he immediately grabbed the hand of the servile girl, repositioning the parasol. Without warning the back of his open hand lashed up and caught her a vicious slap across the face, making her gasp and stagger a little. Rolf then whacked his crop against the side of a shiny boot, before turning back to the prisoners and continuing his sinister address.

'Any prisoner attempting escape will be executed. Be sure about that. Disobedience, slackness or shirking of duties is also punishable. You are our prisoners and you will earn your keep. Numerous electronic defences cover the ground surrounding the camp. Very few have ever managed to escape the compound, and those that have were soon disintegrated to make very fertile manure.' He scanned the disorderly ranks for any signs of a response to his chilling warning.

'You will now be inspected,' he continued, feeling slightly disappointed that none of them had already cracked under his threats; usually one or two broke down and begged his mercy, even at this early stage, and he liked that. 'So I'll leave you in the capable hands of my two assistants.'

'Right, you animals, before you strip out of those rags, I'll have you in two lines facing each other – here and here,' bellowed Stone, pointing to the dust. 'Contact between the sexes will in future be totally forbidden. Move it, into lines,' he shouted, swishing his crop

154

through the air, 'then drop your kit… go!'

The tired captives scrambled into position and shrugged off their uniforms, dropping them to form small piles at their feet.

While the rotund Rolf struggled awkwardly into a waiting seat, assisted by his nubile slave, Koolin and Stone slowly approached the lines of misery.

Koolin thumbed through her electronic clipboard as she counted the prisoners.

'Stand up straight, you sloppy rabble!' snapped Stone. He couldn't suppress his sadistic instincts and lashed his crop down across Rose's hip, leaving a red line of pain across the smooth paleness and making her howl. It had the required result, for the others instantly straightened themselves up as ordered.

Liz impotently clenched her fists by her sides; she couldn't bear to see one of her crew treated so brutally. The urge to step forward and protest on Rose's behalf was strong, but Liz held herself in check, knowing that such an intervention would be a grave mistake. She glanced fleetingly from the corner of her eye as the assaulted girl blinked back a tear, hoping she too could show restraint.

'Did that hurt?' Stone enquired, almost amiably.

'Y-yes,' Rose gasped, her bravery waning and the tears beginning to meander down her cheeks.

The whip cut down again. Rose squealed and futilely tried to protect herself as a second weal lifted on her hip.

'You will show proper respect,' he hissed, jabbing his face within centimetres of hers. 'You address a staff member as sir or ma'am.'

Then he moved further down the line and stood in front of Liz, his eyebrows raised quizzically.

'Commander Elizabeth Hartley, sir,' she responded to his unspoken question.

'A quick learner, and beautiful too,' he murmured, slowly reaching towards her. Hatred for the despicable man simmered in the pit of her stomach and her flesh crawled as he nonchalantly weighed her breasts, the nipples hardening treacherously. She saw, with shame and disgust, a hand of the seated Rolf moving furtively in a trouser pocket as he closely watched the lurid scene, the corner of one beady eye twitching. His free hand slid shamelessly between the thighs of the girl by his side. She remained stock still, holding the parasol over him.

Stone smiled, scarcely able to take his eyes off the feast before him.

Then Koolin interrupted, ready for her first roll call. 'Right, you'll each confirm your name as I stand before you,' she announced, briskly indicating to Stone that he should follow her to the end of the first line.

Each prisoner in turn gave the required information and carefully used the correct form of address.

Soon it was Liz's turn.

'You're a bit of a prize possession here, Hartley,' Koolin purred smugly. 'I've seen that pretty face on many a wanted poster.' Her crop suddenly scorched across the tips of Liz's exposed breasts, making her whimper and double up. It was an agonising and brutal assault. But, as though someone had flicked a switch, Koolin's mood immediately softened and she gently cupped and lifted Liz's chin, straightening her beautiful captive up, her fingers brushing away the tears of anguish that sparkled on her dark eyelashes.

'It seems then, my pretty little prisoner, that I must make an example of you. Tonight, therefore, you will be flogged in the courtyard before the whole camp. It'll be a good example for your colleagues to take note of and learn from.'

The pair moved on, and left Liz trying to digest the knowledge and injustice of an impending public punishment. She was too preoccupied to notice the glazed expression in Rolf's eyes as he rose urgently and ushered the dainty girl back into the building from whence they'd come. As they disappeared through the door he was already unbuckling his belt and loosening his ill-fitting trousers.

At last the roll call was over and Koolin and Stone once again stood together, scanning their bedraggled charges.

Stone nodded once, and a guard roared, 'You will now run around the courtyard! We'll direct you into the medical block when we're ready to search and examine you! Now run, get a sweat on, the doctor will want to check your stamina and heart-rate.'

Twenty prisoners, each holding their discarded uniforms above their heads, ran naked around the perimeter, much to the amusement of the jeering guards. Liz also felt the hungry eyes of their fellow prisoners, in work gangs, feasting on the new flesh parading before them.

They were finally directed into a brick building. After being herded inside they had to discard the clothing in a pile and form two lines, male and female, before small desks. A bored looking unshaven man sat awaiting the women. The only thing that suggested he might be a medic was a white smock. As he picked some remains of his last meal from between his teeth and inspected it another guard had them clasp their hands behind their necks while he frisked them, his glee evident as his rubber-gloved hands slid methodically over and into them. It was a pretty unnecessary procedure, but it further added to their dehumanisation; a useful mechanism for breaking them down still further.

'Name and date of birth?' the medic asked with indifference as each girl was made to step forward in turn. Then they had to lean over the desk, fill out a brief form, and move on to another desk, behind which sat a bespectacled clerk.

After stating their surnames to him they were each given a prisoner number. Two guards then held them while a third pressed an electric brand into their arm. Liz's bore the figure twelve forty-eight, and even she found her stoicism waning as the buzzing needle perforated her flesh. Although she knew that medical techniques could easily remove it, the symbolism wasn't lost on her. Recognising that this processing procedure was gradually wearing even her down, she seriously feared for the resolve of her crew. Some of them were stores accountants or cooks, and had never had to endure the sort of training she'd received to learn how to mentally combat such treatment. Already most were moving as though in a daze. She could see they were physically and mentally drained. The camp's regime was already wearing them down with relative ease.

Next, each girl was called behind a curtain, and when a red-faced Rose emerged Liz's number was called and she had to slip inside. She was now isolated from her companions, trapped in the cubicle with a thin sweating man in a white coat and with a stethoscope around his neck. He wore thick-lens glasses. His lizard-like appearance made Liz even more conscious of her vulnerable nudity, and a shiver of cold dread ran down her spine. And to make things even worse, a door opened beside a medical couch and the lecherous figure of Rolf slithered in.

He wanted to ensure he witnessed the examination of the most beautiful prisoner it had ever been his pleasure to welcome to his camp. He knew from her file how proud and headstrong she was. Breaking her would be a truly memorable moment in his proud career.

And after that?

Well, he had ways of making her and her files

disappear – and she would belong to him. And what a delicious pet she would make!

Liz was told to reach up and grip a rail above her head, and warned not to let go until ordered. The white-coated lizard moved close to her and pressed a combined thermometer/body analyser between her lips. He then shuffled behind her and ordered her to relax her bottom. When she refused to react he gave her buttocks a sharp smack, making her yelp softly and jerk forward a little, and before she could gather herself he'd slipped another similar instrument between the fleshy cheeks and into her rectum.

Liz blushed before the leering figure of Rolf and the busy figure of the doctor, her humiliation intense. Then she closed her eyes and moaned quietly as the doctor's latex-encased fingers roamed freely over her body – prodding and weighing and measuring. He muttered to himself the whole time. Frequently he stopped to remove his glasses and wipe them, although it seemed to be more of a habitual reaction than a necessary one.

Rolf had to adjust his position a little to ease the straining ache in his trousers as the doctor removed and quickly monitored the instruments, and then told the mouth-watering morsel to let go of the bar and hop onto and lie back on the couch. The doctor then wheeled a set of stirrups into position and lifted her feet into the waiting cups.

As he strapped them there Rolf feared he might embarrass himself in his underwear, so enticing was

160

the promise of the pleasures the prisoner was going to provide for him whenever he wanted. He caught his breath as latex fingers delved into her sex, which opened for the intrusive digits like a beautiful orchid. He then watched her back arch just a fraction as the doctor leaned a little closer, pressed a straightened finger against her anus, skewered it a little to gain entrance, and then sank it inside until his palm cupped her intimately.

Thankfully, for Liz, the lizard doctor was quickly finished and apparently satisfied with the examination. Rolf cleared his throat, told the doctor he was doing a fine job, and then slipped away via the same door he'd used to arrive.

With what little dignity she had left in tatters, Liz was dismissed from the hateful cubicle and taken through to a large shower room. The steaming spray of water was a heavenly relief after such an awful day, and after the hot air jets had dried her she was given a different uniform. It fitted pretty tightly, highlighting the voluptuous contours of her body, but at least it was freshly laundered and felt good. She was then led to a cell.

And as the heavy door closed she knew she was now nothing more than prisoner twelve forty-eight – and she belonged to Rolf and his sadistic sidekicks.

'Punishment parade for prisoner twelve forty-eight!' bawled a senior guard as Stone and Koolin, each carrying a vicious whip with many knotted thongs, stepped into the circular arena formed by the gathered prisoners and guards. 'The prisoner will receive twelve strokes, and the punishment will stand as a warning to you all!'

Liz's hair had been pinned up into a bun so as not to obscure her back; the target for the whips. Sweat coated her skin, despite the chill night air.

The scene was illuminated by the camp's many bright perimeter lights, and she bit down on the gag in her mouth as she caught the evil eye of Rolf, staring down upon her from a high chair. Although she desperately wanted to struggle against the bonds that held her wrists and ankles to the whipping frame, she was determined to give the monster as little satisfaction as possible, and so she remained passive, concentrating on breathing slowly and controlling the panic that threatened to overwhelm her.

He nodded without taking his eyes from her trussed body, and she heard Stone and Koolin move closer behind her.

Although she braced herself as best she could, the tension visibly knotting her shoulders, arms and legs, nothing could have prepared her for the flames of agony which scorched across her back with that terrible first stroke. Initially there seemed to be a delayed reaction and she remained silent and taut, straining up on tiptoe. But then the pain gripped and her head fell back as she groaned into the gag and yanked on the immovable leather bonds. She sagged a little, fearing she would not be able to endure the rest of the punishment; that she would be letting her watching people down if she couldn't. A battle of wills was afoot, and Liz knew the odds were stacked heavily and unfairly against her. She knew she couldn't win.

There was another whistle of leather cutting through the still air and she instinctively steeled herself. The breath hissed from between clenched teeth as her rigid body arched in a band of tension, trying to absorb the latticework of fire that now erupted across both cheeks of her bottom. Her hands clenched into balls, desperate to tear themselves away from the bonds and comfort her ravaged flesh… and then to pound into the arrogant faces of Koolin and Stone.

Groaning, Liz slumped again.

The remaining ten strokes melted into a blur of agony, and she was barely aware when the ordeal was over. There was a stunned hush hanging over the watching prisoners, and most of them gazed down at the dusty ground or shuffled their feet. Even some of the guards looked a little disconcerted by the ferocity of the punishment, and avoided the proud looks cast around by the heavily breathing Koolin and Stone.

The leather straps were at last loosened and Liz folded into the arms of two guards, her head lolling back as they picked her up and carried her towards the medical block, a pathway being cleared through the silent prisoners by more of the guards.

Chapter Fifteen

Liz saw the smiling faces of Harry and her parents beyond the tall gates. It was over, she merely had to turn that lock and—

'Wait! You're having a random search, twelve forty-eight.' The vicious little Stone had suddenly appeared at her side, just as she was metres from freedom.

Liz saw the sickened looks of her loved ones as she stood, fingers obediently clasped behind her neck, as his vile hands roamed over her, crudely mauling her breasts through the prison tunic as he leered at Harry and her parents through the fence. Then those hands crawled over her hips and round to her bottom.

'What's this?' With a frown he found and removed the scrap of paper she'd hidden in the waistband of her uniform bottoms. He unfolded it and gazed quizzically at the sequence of numbers scrawled on it, all neatly divided into two. 'Smuggling this out, eh?' he said gleefully. 'Then it's back inside for you.'

Liz was aware of Harry and the others calling her name, clawing frantically at the fence just metres away, but unable to help her. With fingers still locked behind her neck, her continuing status as a prisoner clear, she had to march back to captivity.

Still she heard her name being called. With a jolt she

awoke to Rose gently shaking her shoulder. Since being discharged from the medical centre a few days before, she had been sharing a small cell with Rose and Alice.

It was five three-zero in the morning, and time for their cell to be unlocked. With a hefty electronic clunk the door slid open and a female entered. The girls were a little surprised, but quickly formed a line. A menacing guard filled the open doorway.

'I am the block orderly,' the crop-haired woman announced. 'And you are?'

Each of the girls quoted their numbers in turn.

'Ah yes,' she said pensively, studying Liz. 'Feeling better now, twelve forty-eight?' she asked, as though Liz had merely been a little ill, rather than cruelly beaten for absolutely nothing.

'Yes, miss,' she answered. 'Thank you, miss.'

The woman nodded, but said no more on the matter. She made a brief inspection of the cell, and then turned back to the three girls.

'You will wash and dress now, proceed to the mess hall for your morning intake of food, and then report for working duties in…' she checked her time-piece, 'twenty-four minutes – at six zero-zero hours.'

'Move it you lazy scum,' ordered Koolin, as Liz and Cathy struggled to carry a huge plank the several hundred metres to the construction site within the camp. 'We haven't got all day.'

For several hours Liz and the others had been

performing the gruelling work without a break. Sweat darkened their prison uniforms and the material stuck to their backs and between their breasts and buttocks, and plastered hair to foreheads and cheeks. Koolin, however, lounged with Stone in the shade, talking and laughing together, fanning themselves against the morning heat and enjoying cigars and iced drinks.

Hands more used to the touch of a console keyboard or flying a sub-light interceptor were having to prize the heavy wood from it's hugging embrace with the ground; having probably laid in position for months the earth was reluctant to give the planks up. Gasping with the strain, the two girls slowly managed to ease the next burden up, until Liz staggered and dropped it.

Koolin and Stone fell silent.

Liz looked up anxiously as Koolin put her drink down and stood up, a look of incredulity on her face. 'What the…?'

She strode purposefully towards the crouching prisoner, the butt of a cigar clamped between her teeth, and without warning aimed a vicious kick to her ribs. Liz groaned and keeled over into the dust, clutching her side. The rest of the camp stopped working and the general hubbub about the place faded away. Liz lay in pain for a few moments beneath the harsh sun, then tried to get up, managing to get onto her hands and knees. But Koolin snatched the quirt from her belt and lashed it down across her victim's back.

'Aaahh…!' Liz moaned, barely able to keep a lid on

her simmering anger. 'Sorry… miss,' she gasped, clenching her fists. 'I don't mean to disappoint you. I will try harder—'

'Damned right you'll try harder, you scum!' Koolin hollered, her eyes flashing insanely.

Since arriving at the camp Liz hadn't seen the woman lose it in such a way; she looked almost unstable.

'You hate me, don't you Hartley?!' she screamed, in her rage forgetting to use Liz's number.

Liz rested her forehead in the dust, took a deep breath and counted to ten. Koolin was goading her, and she knew it would be dangerous to react.

'Come on, scum,' the bating continued. 'Tell me you hate me. Tell me you want to see me dead. Tell everybody here how much you want to see me dead. I want to hear you say it! *Say it*!!'

Liz looked up, the sweat stinging her eyes, and saw Koolin stooping over her, her face flushed with fury. She heard Stone giggle from his place in the shade.

'Well?' Koolin persisted. 'Are you not going to admit it? Hah! Not so brave now, are we, Federation scum?' The fact that Liz was floundering in the scorched dirt while the woman stood over her with a weapon raised in her fist seemed to escape the oppressor's attention. The quirt lashed down again and Liz tried in vain to fend off the attack with a raised arm. 'On your feet, damn you!'

Liz struggled onto her knees, rubbing her forearm where the quirt had struck, and then, as Koolin stood eyeing her savagely, she managed to get to her feet.

She swayed on unsteady legs beneath the relentless sun, wondering what was going to happen next, and gradually a thought occurred to her. This confrontation could be the perfect opportunity to lift the spirits of her demoralised crew and all the other prisoners. It might end in her having to accept a painful lesson, but it was surely worth a go. And anyway, she'd had enough of the sadistic dyke!

'So you think you're tough, do you?' Koolin incited, seeing the grim determination in the prisoner's face. 'Well, we'll see about that, shall we? How about a little fight, just you and me? And then you'll see real tough. And if you're as cowardly as I suspect you are and refuse to fight, I'll select two prisoners – and take great pleasure in flogging them!'

All the guards were now paying attention to the showdown, interrupting conversations to watch how things would unravel.

And prisoners laid down tools of toil, those emotionally close to Liz looking up to the cloudless sky in silent prayer that she'd do nothing foolhardy.

Maybe if Liz had been in peak condition she might have stood some semblance of a chance. Her training would have stood her in good stead. But she was underfed, feeling exhausted from the gruelling work, winded from the kick, had no heavy boots or weapons with which to defend or attack, and stood no real chance.

But she nodded, silently accepting the challenge, and her quick reactions did allow her to parry a few surprisingly fast attacks from the pirate, and she even had the satisfaction of delivering a few brief counter-strikes. But they were ineffective, and merely made Koolin laugh and tease her to try harder. Liz lunged, but Koolin easily side-stepped the move and sank rapid punches into her ribs as she lost balance and stumbled a little, the punches accurately targeting the area already weakened by the boot. As Liz staggered past her opponent a heavy boot swung into her bottom and sent her sprawling to the ground.

Many of the prisoners looked away, unable to watch the humiliation of their leader.

Another kick thudded into Liz's side and she curled into a tight ball, cringing under the pain and trying to catch a breath. Dust filled her mouth as she desperately tried to inhale. She could taste blood.

'Come on, scum!' rasped Koolin as she twisted fingers into Liz's hair and wrenched her back up to her feet. 'Get up and fight,' she hissed into Liz's ear, holding her from behind in a crushing embrace. 'Or are all you Federation scum so feeble?'

Koolin's large hands cupped Liz's breasts and she leered at the watching prisoners. 'Your former leader is nothing more than a loose tart,' she shouted. 'Look how she lets me touch her up. She's a tart and she belongs to me!' To emphasise her point she slowly licked up the side of Liz's hot face in a sickening display of possessiveness.

Liz took the split second of an opportunity to draw a deep breath and steady herself. She sensed the woman relax – just a fraction. Koolin pushed her away and held her at arm length, her fingers still gripping her hair and the whip rising slowly in her free hand. The guards and prisoners watched, waiting for the vicious leather to sweep down and inflict its brand of agony across Liz's back. But, calling upon every ounce of what little strength remained, Liz seized the moment and swung round, her fist hooking upward towards the chin of Koolin. Just as her knuckles were centimetres from their target Koolin swayed with deceptive agility out of the danger zone, and as Liz's momentum again carried her off balance Koolin retaliated with a bone-shattering punch to the side of Liz's head.

Liz looked at the pirate for a split second, surprise in her eyes, and then her knees buckled. As she dropped another clubbing blow thumped into her chin, snapping her head back, and she crumpled to the ground, a cloud of dust billowing out around her.

As Stone giggled and applauded Koolin turned slowly, surveying the silent onlookers. 'Let that be a lesson to you all,' she shouted, her own tunic darkening with sweat and her breasts swelling as she slowed her breathing.

She nudged the limp form at her feet with a boot, sneering with disdain. 'None of you are any match for us, so accept your lowly position in Detention Camp

Six. You are all the lowest of the low—' the boot nudged again '—and here's your proof. Prisoner twelve forty-eight came here with a reputation for being a brave fighter, but I've easily put that into context.'

She started to walk back to where Stone sat beaming under the shade, leaving the defeated form of Liz where she lay.

'So we'll have no more nonsense from any of you, or you'll get the same treatment!' Koolin bellowed as she sat down again, and then she quenched her thirst with the iced contents of the glass passed to her by her admiring companion.

'But next time I won't be so lenient,' she added, after wiping her mouth on her sleeve. 'Now get on with your work… *Now*!'

The guards snapped into action and ordered the prisoners back to their labours. An increasingly sombre mood settled over the demoralised wretches, and apart from a few concerned glances at the unmoving shape of Liz, they obediently turned back to their toils.

Chapter Sixteen

'For attacking a guard of Detention Camp Six, prisoner twelve fifty-one is hereby sentenced by this hearing to be removed from here and despatched to our labour mines, where she will work and remain for the rest of her natural days,' announced Rolf.

There were gasps of shock, and Liz could hardly believe her ears. It was a few days after her fight, and still feeling a little bruised and tender – mentally and physically – she knelt with the others before a dais, upon which sat the hatefully pompous figures Rolf, Stone and Koolin. To the side of them poor Helen Swale stood with her hands cuffed together, a numb expression on her bewildered face.

'Any comments or pleading for clemency before sentence is carried out?' Rolf enquired. He was enjoying himself immensely.

Liz knew she just had to do something, but the prospect of exposing herself to yet more abuse filled her with dread. There was a long tense pause and then, closing her eyes and offering up a silent prayer, she spoke up.

'Yes, please, sir,' she said quietly, her voice faltering a little.

'Eh?' Rolf looked around, trying to see who'd

spoken, and then he smiled with anticipatory pleasure as his beady eyes settled on Liz. 'Did you say something, twelve forty-eight?'

Liz opened her eyes and held him with the steadiest stare she could muster. 'Yes sir, I did,' she said, secretly wishing, for the first time ever, that somebody else could for once take the responsibility from her. 'I said, please don't punish her. We're all soldiers serving the Federation and we have rights under normal intergalactic rules of—'

'Ha!' Rolf snorted derisively. 'You gave up any so-called rights when you unwisely chose to attack our territory. Discipline here must be maintained, and this person,' he waved dismissively towards Helen, 'has lacked any degree of discipline whatsoever. An example must be set to the others or chaos will descend. And I will not tolerate that in my camp.'

'Please have mercy, sir,' Liz persisted. 'I... I can tell you're a compassionate man,' she almost choked at having to attach such an emotion to such a sadistic animal, 'and so I ask you again to reconsider.'

Rolf deliberated for a while. He enjoyed the idea of being labelled compassionate, even though the hesitant delivery of the compliment made its sincerity somewhat questionable. 'Yes, I am a compassionate man,' he decided, 'but I hardly think the extent of my benevolence has any relevance to the issue in question. The prisoner assaulted one of my guards, striking without provocation. I simply cannot allow such

173

disgraceful behaviour to go unpunished.'

'Please, sir.' Liz was getting desperate. She'd heard about the dreaded labour mines, and couldn't sit back and allow Helen to be taken away to one of them. 'The guard had provoked her and then punished her excessively and unfairly—'

'I cannot be responsible for the youthful exuberance of my guards,' Rolf interrupted. 'But I must protect them from savages such as you.'

'Let me speak to her, sir. She'll learn to behave, just give her another chance. She'll learn to behave, I promise.'

Once again Rolf deliberated, and turned to whisper to Stone and Koolin in turn. Eventually he made a decision and spoke again.

'I am not a savage, twelve forty-eight. Indeed, I like to agree with you that I'm a reasonable man—' Liz had to bite her lip to prevent herself from saying something she'd regret '—but if you demand my leniency you must at least meet me halfway and offer an alternative solution to this predicament.

'Perhaps, for example, you would put yourself forward to be punished? Perhaps you're prepared to share the blame and the pain?' He chuckled at his own clever use of words, and Stone and Koolin politely laughed too – until the mirth vanished from his face and he held up a hand to silence them.

Liz hesitated for a moment, and then said, 'Yes, sir… if that's what it takes, I will. But you must spare her.'

Rolf was a little surprised, and a little unsettled, by her courageous resolve. 'Very well,' he said, and then turned to Koolin. 'Have twelve forty-eight prepared in my rooms. I think I'll deal with this matter personally.'

In spite of the unpleasant prospect of having to endure some of Rolf's questionable predilections, Liz sighed quietly with relief. 'Thank you, sir,' she conceded deferentially, although her spirits soared, for she had gained a small victory.

The tension of the hearing finally got to Helen Swale, for she swooned and collapsed into the arms of the guard standing just behind her.

And Rolf was looking forward to teaching Hartley a lesson and enjoying himself at the same time. But as he gazed down upon the beauty's kneeling form he also felt, for some inexplicable reason, a chilling sense of foreboding run down his spine.

Liz knelt with her knees spaced wide apart, her ankles and thighs strapped to rings in the floor and her arms bound and stretched out to either side, horizontal to the floor. More chains running from ceiling and floor and fastened to a neck collar kept her head in one position. The whole array of constraints prevented her body moving from its inviting position. She was naked, and a blindfold ensured she was completely disorientated.

After a seemingly endless wait, Liz heard a door swing open and hollow footsteps echoing over the stone floor. Her exposed flesh crawled with dread. She was unable to control the chillingly unpleasant sensation, despite knowing that her obvious trepidation would increase the excitement Rolf would be feeling.

The master of the abominable camp paced around for a while, savouring his moment and savouring the view of the beauty trussed and helpless for his delectation.

'I hope you're ready for me, twelve forty-eight,' he eventually said, enjoying the way her head moved to the sound of his voice. 'I've heard *such* good things about you, and I'd hate to be disappointed; I get extremely angry when someone or something disappoints me.'

'Y-yes, sir,' she managed, despite the nausea churning in her stomach.

He stood a while longer in front of her, thoughtfully rubbing his chin whilst studying the lithe form as he might a fine work of art in a gallery. A small whip made up of leather strips dangled from his free hand. All the while he stayed remote, refraining from touching her, enjoying and prolonging the promise of what was to come. Certainly he'd never had such a breathtaking beauty in his clutches before, and he intended to extract as much pleasure from his good fortune as he could. In addition to her physical beauty and the prospect of enjoying that, he was relishing the prospect of having such an icon of the enemy obeying his every command and bending to his will.

Liz waited, the tension making it difficult for her to breathe. For the umpteenth time she pulled gently on the straps holding her, testing them; but not so much as to give the man any pleasure from her evident desire to be freed. She wasn't too sure where he was, but she sensed he was standing in front of her, watching – tormenting.

Rolf moved. The breath caught anxiously in Liz's chest and she jerked her head slightly to one side, blindly following the sound of his slow, crisp footsteps as he circled his prey.

He stood quietly again, admiring the delicious rear view; sculptured shoulders draped by lustrous dark hair, the downward sweep of her back, the flair of her hips to a luscious bottom, toned thighs leading to shapely calves and neat feet.

Rolf slowly raised his arm and held the whip aloft. He gazed down at the mouth-watering target for a few more seconds, and then swept the whip down across the prisoner's buttocks. The fleshy globes quivered under the impact. The bonds creaked and rattled quietly as her body jerked. She stiffened and her back arched as the breath hissed between her clenched teeth. A red weal rose as the whip lifted again, and Rolf drank in the sight.

He moved his feet slightly to ease the discomfort forming in his trousers. 'Did that hurt, twelve forty-eight?' he whispered menacingly.

Liz could not even begin to defy him or deny him his

sadistic pleasure by pretending it didn't. She nodded weakly, wondering just how much punishment he intended to subject her to, and just how much she'd be able to take; since being held at the camp her body had already suffered much at the hands of Koolin and Stone.

Rolf's upper body swivelled again, his arm and the whip followed, and the small room was once more filled with the sound of leather cutting into firm flesh and the whimpers of the trussed prisoner.

Rolf could no longer contain himself and abandoned the delights to be had by tormenting her, and instead set to beating her with a steady rhythm. Liz gasped again and again as the stripes of heat seared into her back and buttocks. She tried to writhe away from the incessant blows, but it was hopeless; Stone and Koolin had done an excellent job in securing her.

Rolf began to breathe heavily as the effort got to his unfit body. His trousers tented at the groin, and beads of sweat ran down the sides of his chubby face. The beating was relentless. Rolf became almost frenzied. His chins quivered with the effort of every strike. Liz lost count of the blows she'd suffered, her determination to defy the brute evaporating as her whimpers and grunts gave way to pitiful wails for mercy.

At last there was a lull. The stuffy room was filled with the sounds of heavy staccato breathing rasping in his chest and her miserable sobs.

Through a haze of confusion and whirling emotions Liz heard the whip clatter to the stone floor, a rustle of clothing, and she knew full well what was coming next.

Rolf, his excitement so intense his legs felt a little weak, opened his trousers and shuffled around to stand before her red face. Smudged tears trickled down from beneath the blindfold and glistened on her cheeks and chin. For a moment he admired Stone's and Koolin's capabilities – and mentally praised himself for being such a good tutor – as he acknowledged the way her head was bound, affording easy access to his whims.

He gripped his erection in his fist, enjoying the feel of his pulsing masculinity, and moved closer.

'Be a good prisoner now, my dear,' he panted. Eyes bulging as he watched, his bulbous helmet touched those lovely soft lips and she instinctively snatched her head back the minute distance the bonds would allow, as though being scolded by something hot. 'Open up for me,' he urged quietly, his penis following her.

Liz knew resistance was utterly hopeless. The man represented everything she loathed about the enemy, but she stiffened her resolve, reminding herself that this was an act of sacrifice to protect a persecuted member of her crew. Gradually her spirits rose; hers was an act of valour, whereas Rolf's was the behaviour of a depraved animal, and completely epitomised the differences between her nation and his. Suddenly she could sense another victory.

She *would* give Rolf some of what he craved; he could have her body.

But he could never have her soul.

And in submitting to him she would prove herself strong enough to endure his depravities, and he would expose both to her and to himself his damnable weaknesses.

Liz opened her mouth.

Rolf smiled broadly and pushed his hips forward. He shuddered with delight as his erection touched her moist lips, forced them wider, and eased into the snug confines of her warmth. The veined underside forged along the cushion of her tongue until his tip nudged the back of her throat. He gazed down at the top of her lovely head, felt the blindfold and her silky fringe touch the underhang of his belly, and then closed his eyes to savour the moment.

The bonds creaked again as he set about a steady rhythm, careful not to overdo it and risk bringing such a victorious moment to a premature and disappointing conclusion. The clammy warmth in the dank room increased. As he moved he removed his tunic. He was sweating heavily as he gripped her head and guided her back and forth, savouring the sensations of her mouth and the sounds of her suckling.

'You're enjoying this, twelve forty-eight...' he grunted.

Despite her abhorrence of the man, Liz couldn't deny the frisson of excitement the stiff penis plugged inside her mouth induced deep in her stomach. She didn't respond in any particular way, but continued to suck and lick as best she could; for some reason she was now determined to prove to the man she really was everything he'd ever fantasised about; that Federation girls really were beyond compare.

'That's enough,' Rolf suddenly croaked, withdrawing from her. 'We don't want to spoil this momentous liaison, now do we?' He watched as Liz instinctively licked her lips. 'Besides,' he went on, 'there's another of your delightful little openings I want to enjoy.'

He moved awkwardly, looking totally ungainly; naked, with his trousers around his boots and his erection waving beneath his corpulent girth. He waddled around her and between her outspread feet, the sight of her vulnerable beauty making his penis lurch and almost ruining the moment.

Taking a deep breath and calming himself, he knelt on the stone floor.

Liz tensed as stubby fingers crawled up her inner thighs and, with no finesse or consideration for her, plunged into her sex. Her hips dipped a little as he clumsily explored, his fingers squelching in her gripping depth.

'You *are* enjoying this,' he mumbled again, as though to himself. 'By fuck, but you're a sexy little bitch,' he hissed, and then Liz caught her breath as his bloated helmet eased between her sex lips and his stiff cock sank into her, spreading and penetrating. Her excitement mounted, and she desperately wanted the bonds to disappear so she could move, as she really wanted to. And Rolf was working hard behind her, rutting against her punished bottom with vigorous stabs of his groin, drawing her closer and closer to an orgasm. But just at the moment when she succumbed completely to the pirate and suppressed the last tattered remnants of her mental resistance, he withdrew.

Liz was left feeling empty, and his quiet chuckling of satisfaction filled her with shame. But her emptiness was instantly forgotten as she felt his hands move from her hips, grip her burning buttocks, thumbs prise them apart, and then his lubricated cock pressed beyond her tight anus and sank into her rear passage. For a moment her discomfort was intense. But then her insides melted, and as the pirate found his rhythm she groaned her encouragement. He leaned across her sore and tensed back and whispered goading obscenities into her ear – mocking her. But his abuse merely enflamed her further. As her orgasm engulfed her straining body and mind Rolf could resist the moist clutches of her bottom no longer and erupted inside her.

He wilted onto her back, making her whimper as the muscles in her arms strained to take his considerable weight and the bonds bit into her wrists. He smiled lazily; oh, how sweet victory was – and how sweet Hartley's fit young body was. He promised himself a lot more fun with her in the future.

After he'd straightened his clothing he stood gloating over Liz's limp form, and told her she now had to be nice to a very special guest of his. And if she didn't co-operate Swale's original punishment would be restored.

After a slap to her nearest flank he bent, picked up the whip, savoured the sight of her for one last time, and then left her blindfolded and alone.

Liz recovered slowly, the throbbing in her poor bottom and back a constant companion. She wondered fearfully what horrors awaited her now. She was feeling exhausted and confused, and didn't know what to think about what had just happened with Rolf. Should she register it as a mental victory, or had he won? Was she merely fooling herself by trying to perceive her lusty participation as anything other than the act of a traitorous whore? As she knelt alone in the humid silence she began to see Rolf as the victor, and began to berate herself for being so stupidly naïve.

But her self-torture was abruptly cut short as she heard the door quietly open and close. Footsteps moved slowly across the floor towards her. 'Who – who's there?' she asked timidly, turning her head to try to follow the movement of the unknown newcomer. 'Please... who are you?' she pleaded again, her concerns mounting.

She could hear faint breathing, as though the stranger was trying to stalk her without disclosing his or her whereabouts. But Liz, using the deprivation of sight to increase the acuteness of her hearing, knew the person was in front of her.

She heard a belt being unbuckled, and suspected the phantom was a man. Material rustled and she knew it was a pair of trousers being lowered, and then knees creaked, something smoothly soft yet firm touched her lips, and her perception was confirmed.

Fingers curled into her hair to hold her firm, more fingers dug into her cheeks to prise her mouth open, and then a column of gnarled flesh forged inside, and for the second time in a short space of time she was fellating one of the enemy.

The breathing above her grew heavier and quickened. The fingers left her face and joined the others, where they pulled her head back and forth vigorously. The aggressive movement made her breasts swing and they rubbed against thick hairy thighs that quivered, betraying her violator's intense degree of excitement.

Without warning the knotted flesh plopped audibly from between her wet lips. The fingers disentangled from her hair and huge paws mauled her breasts, and then wrapped them around the spearing cock. The man grunted as he started to rut against Liz's bound torso, fucking her deep cleavage.

'Pluh-please…' she stammered, as the brutish phantom used her body to masturbate against. 'Wh-who are you…?' But her timid question was answered by a gruff chuckle. There was something she recognised – something that made her abused flesh crawl – but she couldn't put her finger on it.

The column of flesh ploughing up and down between her breasts pulsed and swelled, and even though she couldn't see it, she knew the man was close to

184

ejaculating. His movements became increasingly erratic and his demanding grunts became more and more urgent. The fingers dug into her breasts, making her wince, and moulded the velvety warm globes of flesh tighter around the plunging cock. It nudged up against her throat, leaving a sticky trail on her perspiring skin. And then the man hissed, held still for a few long seconds, and then spattered copiously onto her chest, his viscous fluid oozing down onto the slopes of her breasts. He suddenly snatched away from her. Liz heard a wet rhythmic stroking, and then one hand cupped and raised her face, the wet pumping increased in tempo and Liz tried to recoil as a second eruption spat onto her lips and chin. The man groaned, rested his spongy helmet against her flushed face, and spent again and again until he was utterly drained.

Liz sagged, defeated and deflated, the unknown stranger's salty unguent feeling chilly as it dried on her face, her throat, and her breasts.

'Holy shit!' the man sighed heavily. 'Have I always wanted to do that!'

Liz stiffened again; she knew that voice.

'Yeah…' he chuckled, 'you recognise me now, don't you?' The large clumsy hands molested her exposed breasts again, rubbing his own viscous emission into her flesh. 'You've always considered yourself a superior bitch, haven't you, Hartley? Well, we're not so superior now, are we?'

Liz couldn't believe what she was hearing. She

wanted the floor to open up and swallow her there and then.

'That was good, Hartley,' the voice continued triumphantly, 'but I'm gonna have plenty more fun with you from now on – you mark my words. I've changed sides, and for my co-operation Mr Rolf has promised me as much time with you as I want.'

Liz shook her head in disbelief. How could the blundering idiot have been so stupid as to desert the Federation?

'Yeah, it's me, Hartley… it's McDuff!'

Chapter Seventeen

The following morning Liz was allowed to shower and put on a clean uniform. Then she was taken to see Rolf and – with nothing being said about the previous evening, almost as though nothing had happened – was told she was to be interviewed by a journalist from a neutral planet. He explained that the fate of her crew would depend on her responses, and that she was forbidden to give any information or make detrimental comments about their treatment or living conditions at Detention Camp Six.

Going on, he gave precise details about the conduct expected of her and how she had to be utterly respectful to the interviewer, who was someone very important. If she did not adhere closely to his instructions, she and her crew could expect to suffer severely.

When she was marched into the small room occupied by the elegant seated figure she felt a stomach-churning fear mixed with anger. The darting eyes of Velma Strood swept over her contemptuously.

The stick-like woman was venom personified!

With a shudder, Liz recalled her remarks to the woman a few months before when she'd tried to misquote her during an interview. The look of rage on Velma's face when Liz had slapped her at the subsequent party, and tipped a drink over her, would always remain firmly entrenched in her memory.

Liz sensed it was payback time.

Dressed so plainly, compared to Velma and her expensive suit, Liz stood quietly and obediently in front of the woman, trying to work out the significance of her unexpected appearance.

Velma's angular features broke into a tight smile as she eyed the lovely creature that had fallen so neatly into her lap. Being a good investigative reporter for over twenty years, and having been into such camps before, she could easily guess what kind of torments Liz and her crew had been having to endure. She also knew Rolf would have forbidden her to tell about it. Her future treatment, and that of her crew, would depend greatly on her behaviour and co-operation during the interview. Understandably the Magellan empire only wanted her to write good publicity. What she actually knew, or thought, didn't really matter; only the story counted. Thinking back to her last encounter with the beautiful young Federation commander, Velma felt a little spark of anticipation.

'So, we meet again, Hartley,' the clipped voice greeted. 'I do hope you're keeping well?'

'Yes… thank you,' Liz stood tall with her shoulders proudly back. 'Well, as best as can be expected – under the circumstances.' She longed to sit – her aching muscles were a testament to the several hours labouring she'd done that day – but she wasn't about to ask permission.

'I hope you like my outfit, Hartley,' the woman continued. 'It's a new one; not so long ago a drink was spilt over one of my favourites.' She smiled tightly, allowing her eyes to drift over the curvaceous figure standing before her.

'Yes, I'm sorry about that misunderstanding, Velma.' Liz attempted some sort of appeasement. 'It had been a bad day.' As much as Liz disliked the woman, Velma Strood was a link, her only link, to the world that lay beyond the boundaries of the hell that was Detention Camp Six. Just perhaps her unexpected arrival would create a hint of an opportunity for Liz to exploit.

'Forget it,' Velma smiled tightly. 'I know these things happen.' She oozed barely concealed spite.

'This is Velma Strood reporting from a prison camp somewhere on Magellan, where some of the crew of the captured Federation raider, *Explorer*, are being held,' she suddenly said into the microphone of the small vid-recorder she held. 'With me is prisoner Elizabeth Hartley, the former second-in-command of the *Explorer*. She is currently undergoing corrective discipline, and yet the vid will show things as they are and help to dispel the wild rumours about savage beatings, and the like, which people often think are inflicted upon the prisoners here.'

Pressing the pause button on the vid she spoke again to Liz. 'Now remember,' she said, 'think carefully about what you say. What I don't like I won't use, you can be sure of that.'

Switching on the machine again she started the interview.

'Elizabeth,' she gushed, as though they were old friends, 'your ship was captured in violation of Magellan space. What was the purpose of your mission here?'

'It was a legitimate mission,' Liz answered firmly. 'We had originally been called upon for help by the Taurions, because certain unknown elements had attacked their trading stations.'

Although the prisoner was dressed in an uncomplimentary uniform and standing subserviently, she still somehow managed, thought Velma, to retain her dignity and give commendable justification during the interview for the actions of *Explorer* and the Federation. Even though she couldn't speak freely, Velma had to admire her guile and guts. The interview wasn't altogether the grovelling apology by a broken warrior that she'd hoped for. Curse the girl, she thought bitterly.

Well she, Velma Strood, would just have to do something to redress the balance and bring Elizabeth Hartley down a peg or two – even if only in private.

Looking at the monitor that evening, Velma watched Liz being taken from her cell by a guard. The delicious prisoner wore only a tight white vest and white panties, the lower and upper extremities of which didn't meet, and so her admirably flat midriff was left bare. With her hands cuffed behind her back the vest was also stretched enticingly across her firmly thrusting breasts, the tension in the material rendering the outline of her nipples clearly definable. And to accentuate her prisoner status a red ball gag distorted her pretty lips and gave her an adorable expression of wide-eyed vulnerability.

Following their progress on the screen, the reporter saw the guard hand his charge over to Koolin. She then readied her vid-recorder as the two females entered the chamber a few minutes later.

As previously agreed, Koolin was naked but was hiding her identity, even though she knew that the film was for Velma's personal collection and delectation. The black leather mask made her presence seem more ominous than ever. She led Liz to two parallel bars running horizontal to the floor between two uprights, before cuffing her ankles, widespread, to each end of the lower one. Briskly, she removed Liz's wrist cuffs, and just as briskly she pulled the tight vest up and off. She then fastened Liz's wrists above her head to each end of the upper bar, to leave her victim spread-eagled and straining up on tiptoe.

Velma licked her lips with relish at the way Liz's breasts sprang free when the vest was roughly removed, and then at the way they flattened slightly under the strain of the stretched position. Then she mirrored and recorded the wicked glint in Koolin's eyes as the masked prison official stood before their beautiful plaything fastening the straps of a large black dildo around her own hips. Then she caught the bewildered look of dread as their victim eyed the monstrous artificial phallus sprouting aggressively from her outrageous ally. The eye and ear of the vid-recorder captured the sensuous scene perfectly.

The muscled form of Koolin sidled closer to the bound beauty. She leaned in and pecked her provocatively on the tip of her nose. She paused, their lips almost touching, gazing into Liz's eyes, and then she reached round, cupped Liz's buttocks, bent her knees a little, and thrust her hips and the plastic stalk up into their plaything's exposed body with one smooth lunge.

The camera zoomed in, catching forever the paradoxical expression of confused loathing and unexpected bliss on Liz's face as she strained up further on tiptoe. Velma could read the indecision whirling around in Liz's head through her body-language; she wanted to strain up away from the monstrous artificial cock, and she also craved to relax and sink down on it to the root. She continued zooming in until the frame was full of Liz's exquisite beauty, her eyes fluttering shut and her head lolling back, her lustrous hair sweeping over her shoulders and down her back.

Velma panned out again and saw the naked buttocks of Koolin clenching and relaxing rhythmically as she thrust deep into her victim. The plastic glistened between their toned bodies every time it withdrew.

Moving round she filmed Liz's hips and bottom instinctively grinding back against her assailant.

Moving in closer she could smell their passion. Liz's mouth was beginning to slacken around the gag with her approaching orgasm. Velma guessed that the tiny clitoral spur on the phallus was doing its work well.

Koolin sniggered and signalled for Velma to get another close-up of Liz's dreamy expression as the girl's muffled gasps told the devious collaborators that she was climaxing… and Velma Strood had it all on film – every delightful second of it!

A few minutes later Velma stood behind the limp form of Liz. She was now naked and wearing the glistening dildo, and Koolin lounged on a chair operating the vid-recorder, one leg slung over the plastic arm and fingers idly toying between her thighs. Velma knew Liz was barely conscious, still swooning from the after-pleasures of her orgasm. She stepped forward, gripped the unresisting hips of the girl, pulled them back slightly to ease her entrance, and then smoothly penetrated the limp form.

Elizabeth Hartley had for a long time been the central participant of Velma's more imaginative sexual fantasies, and at long, long last Velma Strood had the real thing at her mercy and within her arms. She eased her hands reverently around the sumptuous feast, savouring the feel of her warm flesh, and cupped her glorious breasts possessively.

'Oh, how long I've waited for this moment,' she

sighed into Liz's ear; but Liz didn't hear the words of homage, so muddled were her mind and her emotions.

A thin smile lifted the corners of Velma's tight lips as she felt the nipples stiffen beneath her palms. 'Yes…' she encouraged, 'I knew you'd love this.' For a moment Velma luxuriated in the thought of all the people – men and women alike – who would give anything to be where she was now, holding the girl she was holding now. Men didn't interest Velma Strood, they never had. But she'd certainly enjoyed many girls in her time – some of them willing, some of them not so. But never had she enjoyed such a special and rare treat as this. The fact that Elizabeth Hartley was not a lesbian only added to the spice; to corrupt someone so perfectly incorruptible was a truly intoxicating drug.

Her quarry's head lolled back onto her shoulder, and as she massaged the wonderful flesh in her eager hands she kissed the side of her face, her lips feeling the inert ball gag through her delicate cheek. As she did so she gradually increased the tempo of her grinding hips. Liz breathed deeply, and Velma welcomed the twin mounds of flesh that were forced even more firmly into her hands. The girl's dreamy and instinctive pleasure, compounded with the knowledge of what she was doing – and to whom – ensured that Velma could not withstand the myriad of sexual stimulants bombarding her body and mind for long, and as she shuddered in a breathless orgasm she felt Liz stiffen a little and join her in mutual ecstasy.

When Velma Strood was again dressed and had regained her poise, and her vid-recorder from Koolin, she lifted Liz's chin and kissed her lightly on a tear-streaked cheek. 'Whenever I'm feeling a little down or lonely,' she whispered, 'I'll play my treasured film and share our little secret over and over again.'

Chapter Eighteen

Liz felt depressed as she ate her unappetising evening meal of bread, thin stew and food-supplement tablets, whilst reviewing her predicament.

That night was an anniversary of her relationship with Harry and they had planned, some time before, a romantic dinner for two in an exquisite bistro they knew. The ambience of their intended venue couldn't contrast more with her current circumstances. She and the other prisoners ate at long wooden tables and benches in absolute monastic silence, closely monitored by the guards. Instead of soft background music they had to contend with the angry rebuke of any guard catching a prisoner dawdling with his or her food or attempting to communicate with another. Rather than the romantic glow of subdued lighting they sat beneath the harsh white glare of overhead strip lights.

But at least her hands were clean, and perhaps she should accustom herself to being thankful for small mercies – very small mercies.

That morning they had been ingrained with soil from the backbreaking task of planting foodstuffs in the camp's self-sustaining vegetable plots. However, in the afternoon the grime was washed away by detergents and other cleaning agents in the steam and oppressive heat of the camp laundry. For hours Liz had to wash and steam and iron pile upon pile of guard and prisoner uniforms. She reflected that the officers always seemed to be selected for the most physically exhausting and mentally numbing jobs, with the junior ranks generally receiving lighter duties.

But as the guards' shouts indicated the mealtime to be over, Liz consciously switched off that train of thought; it was all part of the divide and rule policy used by the pirates, and a policy she knew better than to succumb to. She was tired and needed to sleep, and thoughts of being locked away in her tiny cell were almost welcoming.

Chapter Nineteen

It was the first roll call of the day, but to the dismay of the bedraggled crew the turncoat, McDuff, was taking it. Clearly revelling in the new power he strolled before and looked up and down each of his former comrades in turn.

'Everything okay, Hartley?' he asked reasonably.

'Yes... sir.' She longed to put her former sergeant in his place, but she knew it would be a big mistake. Apart from the revenge he would take great pleasure in extracting, she had to set an example for the crew.

'I hope you're keeping fit,' he continued, sweating and leering. 'But in case you're not, drop down and give me twenty press-ups.'

Knowing she had little option but to obey, she sank down to the stony dry ground before him.

One of the Federation's most revered females, previously McDuff's superior, was prone at his feet obediently performing the exercises he'd demanded. With impunity he nudged her side with the toe of a boot, demanding more effort as she strained under the hot sun.

For Liz this public humiliation by McDuff was almost as bad as the way he'd abused her when she'd been helplessly blindfolded and bound in the privacy of

Rolf's room. She knew that for some reason he felt he had scores to settle with her; imagined grievances that had for some reason festered and grown out of all proportion over the years. For Liz, life seemed extremely bleak at that precise moment.

McDuff then had her get up and touch her toes, while he stood behind, ogling her flexing buttocks as she dipped from the waist, and crudely urging her on to ever greater efforts. Liz bit her lip against the embarrassment as he stepped closer and spanked her bottom a few times, making a joke out of it to the watching guards. But she knew the useless oaf was getting himself all aroused, and she also knew that could make him dangerous, stirring his naturally sadistic and bullying nature. She wasn't surprised when the spanking turned into furtive, distasteful gropes.

At last McDuff cleared his throat a little and glanced around, as though realising he was perhaps getting a little too carried away and exposing a chink in his armour to anyone watching closely enough, and allowed Liz to straighten up and relax.

Just at that moment the outer door to Rolf's office opened and he strutted out, the lovely girl again following and shading him with the parasol. McDuff hurried to the front of the untidy prisoner ranks and tried to order them into some sort of orderly unit. Rolf stood before the rabble with an air of immense self-importance, and the fool of a traitor bumbled back a few paces, reverently standing just behind his new leader.

'I have just received a message from our hierarchy,' Rolf announced grandly. 'It seems there may be some possibility of a deal being struck between them and your crawling Federation. I am awaiting confirmation, but it seems you are soon to be released from here and returned to your planet. You'll return to your cells now, and tomorrow morning you will travel back to the spaceport.'

And that was it. Without another word Rolf turned and went back inside, immediately followed by the girl.

There was a ripple of hope amongst the ranks, and they even felt confident enough to glance and smile fleetingly at each other, regardless of the watching guards. Chins lifted, backs straightened, and shoulders pulled back as the seed of hope sewn by Rolf's words restored a little of their pride and determination.

Even Liz, knowing better than to fully trust what she'd heard, couldn't totally suppress the feeling of optimism lifting her spirits. And the look of disappointment on McDuff's face as he sensed his quarry being snatched away from him was a joy to behold. He lowered his gaze and shuffled his great feet as Liz fixed him with a venomous stare that told him in no uncertain terms that retribution would be hers.

However, Liz reminded herself to be cautious – their nightmare wasn't over just yet.

Chapter Twenty

'Before you leave us tomorrow, twelve forty-eight, I require your presence at a tiny gathering I have to host this evening. It'll be a little tiresome, but it's one of the duties I have to perform as head of Detention Camp Six.' Liz remembered Rolf's pompous words as she served him and his guests; a haughty woman who was apparently Valdez's wife, travelling with an explosives expert on his way to the spaceport. His knowledge was apparently needed for the hostage hand-over.

As she leant over the dinner table she felt that particular guest's contemptible touch crawling sneakily up the inside of her thigh. The mauling intruder made her jump a little, although such sleaziness was only to be expected by now. She almost spilt the drink she was pouring for Koolin, who was sitting beside the lecherous guest who was now lightly pinching her tender flesh, but she concentrated on her duties as she'd been warned to beforehand by Rolf.

Once the glass was full and she'd received an arrogant nod of approval from Koolin, she moved away and the hand lost contact. As she melted thankfully into the background she remembered again her earlier brief meeting with Rolf. She had been left in no doubt at all as to the penalties she would suffer for any mistakes or accidents whilst serving. And whatever the guests wanted, they got – and that included respect and subservience.

The small hover van, parked in the mess compound behind the kitchen where Liz was disposing of some of the leftovers of the meal, was unguarded. It was the van that had brought the visiting bomb expert, whom she guessed was travelling to the spaceport to advise on the deactivation of *Explorer's* self-destruct system. She wondered if his 'expertise' would be enough to thwart her own little plan.

Liz watched quietly from the shadows just beyond the light spilling out from the open kitchen door, and saw the glowing tip of the driver's cigar and his bulky shadow disappear around a corner, and then heard the soft splattering sounds as he emptied his bladder up against a wall.

As Liz stood in the stillness of the evening, the sudden urge for total revenge was simply too intense for her to ignore. So without considering the consequences, she dashed quietly through the darkness, leaned into the vehicle, instantly put her hand on a small limpet mine, and then ghosted back to the kitchen just as she heard the driver fart loudly and his footsteps returning.

The device nestled so neatly into her palm, and she experienced a sudden surge of adrenaline that she at last had the opportunity to wreak havoc upon the pirate animals and savour the sweet taste of retribution.

For the first time in a long time she was in control.

She had once more gained the initiative over her unsuspecting enemy.

Now committed, she tried to look busy around the kitchen, and when the two cooks were otherwise distracted in yet another arm-waving and pot-throwing argument she carefully hid her little surprise, its diminutive size making concealment relatively easy.

Over the next hour or so, with her destructive little secret hidden in the kitchen, she found it easier to endure the disparaging comments and touching from Rolf, Koolin, Stone, and the other two. Indeed, she struggled to suppress a tiny smile of satisfaction that might just have given her game away.

Gradually, though, the excessive amounts of alcohol the small gathering consumed began to take effect. Rolf grabbed Liz as she was clearing away the last of the dishes and hauled her onto his expansive lap. 'Huh-how about a goodbye kiss for me then, eh?' he slurred. 'It – it's all thanks to me that you're going home tomorrow,' he boasted, inaccurately. 'Don't you think that deserves a little thank you?' His frame wobbled as he burped quietly and his alcohol-laden breath ruffled Liz's fringe. She stiffened, but remained passive as his podgy wet lips clumsily sought and then smothered hers. Fat fingers groped at her breasts and pinched her nipples through her uniform tunic as he slobbered over her, devouring her as though she was the succulent slab of meat he'd just recently consumed.

Valdez's wife sipped her wine and slyly eyed the outline of the nipples budding against the drab material of the prisoner uniform between Rolf's greedy fingers. The generous breasts cosseted within certainly looked nicely firm yet malleable – just how she liked them. She idly touched the rim of her glass with the tip of her tongue, and then sipped a little more wine, plans developing nicely in her head.

She was only at the odious place in the back of beyond because she had to join her husband at the spaceport the next day, but perhaps the dull evening spent with dull company might have its compensations, after all. She drained her glass and lifted it, an eyebrow arched, and watched as the lovely young prisoner extricated herself from the tentacle-like grasp of Rolf. Her pulse quickened as the delectable morsel stood close and poured more of the rich scarlet liquid into her glass, and her nostrils flared as she inhaled the delicious scent of her. The sensual allure of the prisoner was almost easing the pounding of her migraine. The girl's position exposed a tantalising glimpse of her shadowy cleavage, and the teasing shape of her nipples pressing against the tunic could still be enjoyed.

As Liz straightened up a little Sabrina Valdez lightly touched her fingertips to the hand that held the bottle. 'Thank you, my dear,' she purred, as the touch caused Liz to hesitate. For a few seconds Sabrina stared deep into Liz's eyes. The look held her there, while the manicured fingers stroked the back of her hand.

'I didn't realise you had such attractive prisoners here,' Sabrina Valdez said to Rolf, without releasing Liz from her captivating stare. 'Perhaps you'd let me take her to my room tonight, just to keep me company, you understand.'

Liz shuddered at the prospect, but tried not to show her revulsion. Koolin and Stone looked resentful, and the explosives expert looked envious. Rolf's head appeared to be too heavy for his neck as he tried to focus on his female guest, and although somewhat befuddled, he was aware enough to know it would not be wise to disappoint the wife of Valdez. Despite previously planning to wallow in the delights of Elizabeth Hartley for one last time that night, he relented as graciously as his envy would allow, and said, 'Of course, my dear Sabrina… how could I *possibly* refuse such a revered guest?'

Sabrina Valdez smiled. 'Thank you. I'll be sure to tell my husband of your kindness.' She beckoned Liz closer with a thin finger, and whispered in her ear, 'I've had enough of these bores for one evening, and so I'm going to my room now. When you've finished here you'll come to me. Bring a bottle of wine, and don't be too long. I'll be waiting.'

Once she'd swept from the room Liz opened more of the wine and started plying those remaining with as much of it as she could, hoping they wouldn't become suspicious by her sudden eagerness to serve. She could sense Koolin watching her closely, but gradually even her eyes became more and more glazed. Rolf slowly slurred more incoherently and belched more frequently, as did Stone and the explosives expert. Sweaty hands grabbed her more and more intimately as she moved amongst them, but she smiled bravely and made herself available to the vile groping. Rolf hauled her onto his lap again and buried his rosy face into her cleavage. She stroked his head and gently rolled her bottom against the lump she could feel beneath it. Once again he mauled her breasts and kissed the soft upper slopes as her tunic gaped invitingly. The other three occupants of the room watched and drank. The two men adjusted their positions to ease the strain in their trousers, and Koolin pressed a hand between her thighs under cover of the table.

Suddenly Liz was caught slightly unawares as Rolf lurched up onto his feet and spread her back on the table. He forced her legs apart and wormed his paunch between them. Liz had thought him beyond such activity, and watched with loathing as he fumbled heavy-handedly with his trousers. He swayed over her, his eyes barely open. The other three huddled closer to enjoy the erotic scene. Cigar smoke hovered in wavy layers over the table.

Liz closed her eyes and waited... but when she opened them again Rolf seemed to be unconscious on his feet. He remained motionless for a few seconds, the ends of his unbuckled belt in his unmoving hands, and then toppled forward like a felled tree. He slumped, half on her soft body and half on the table, cracking his forehead on the solid surface as he did.

Liz lay squashed beneath his immense weight, and then managed to roll him off and worm herself free, leaving him sprawled and dribbling on the tabletop, whispering endearments to it.

She stood and took the chance to straighten her clothing and gather some degree of composure, and then moved to ply the remaining three with yet more wine. Although they tried collectively to force themselves upon her, she was too sober and they were too drunk to have any realistic chance of succeeding. One by one they succumbed to the affects of the alcohol. Stone and the explosives expert fell into drunken heaps where they sat, and Koolin rose unsteadily and staggered off to her room, banging into the doorframe as she tried to negotiate the exit.

Liz waited for a few minutes, watching and listening. It was late, and apart from the guttural snoring filling the room, all seemed quiet. Quickly, and remaining alert, she dashed to the kitchen, and was relieved to find the two cooks had finished for the night and gone to their quarters. She found the small mine and returned to the dining room. The three drunks were still heavily asleep. Quickly she set the timer for twenty hours ahead, dipped down agilely, and attached the tiny but lethal bomb to the underside of the table, as near in to the centre as she could.

Suddenly feeling totally drained, but also feeling a

weight lifting off her shoulders, she took one last contemptuous look back at the three hateful individuals, and then took a deep breath, picked up yet another bottle of wine, and headed towards the room where Sabrina Valdez waited.

Chapter Twenty-One

Valdez strolled into his private quarters at the spaceport and smiled; the prisoner had been prepared just as he'd demanded.

Liz sat on a chair, her wrists bound to the arms and each ankle bound to a footrest. Another broad strap fitted snugly around her middle, just beneath her breasts, hugging her tightly to the chair back. Despite leaving Detention Camp Six that morning, with the other members of her crew who had been there, she was still dressed in the prison uniform, although the one she wore was at least freshly laundered.

Valdez studied her appreciatively, whilst showing no outward emotion, noting how the broad tightly buckled strap pulled and smoothed the material of her prison tunic enticingly over her defenceless breasts, and accentuated their generous proportions and shape. With her every anxious breath the buttons strained valiantly to contain their hidden merchandise. His narrowed eyes travelled slowly upwards, admiring the beckoning hint of an inviting cleavage, and settled on the collar secured around her slender throat. Finally his gaze alighted on her beautiful face, and although she silently challenged him with a defiant stare, he could read the uncertainty there.

Valdez nodded to Sulin, who had performed her task of securing his bargaining chip admirably.

He turned his attention back to the bound girl, a twinkle of amusement in his eyes, and introduced himself. He noted with some pleasure how she remained impassive, silently challenging his authority, and he felt his penis stiffen a little; this one would add immense enjoyment to the morning's work.

'We have much to do, my dear,' he said smoothly. 'I will shortly let you speak to Harry Clarke, but,' he raised a finger to emphasise his point, 'if you say anything at all out of line...' his smile broadened, 'well, I think you know what to expect.'

The man filled Liz with a sickening cocktail of hatred and dread. Despite his passive demeanour, he oozed danger.

'We are going live, as it were, to the bridge of *Explorer* where Clarke and two of your crew are going to deactivate the self-destruct mechanism for us. We know all about the codes, and if all goes well your ordeals will soon be at an end and we'll return you to Earth with the guarantee of safe passage.'

Liz knew the two others necessary to key in their codes with Harry must be Joanne and Kate – and she'd not had the opportunity to tell Joanne about the need to halve the code numbers.

Valdez sat on a stool beside Liz, flicked a remote control, and relaxed arrogantly as though about to enjoy a movie. A large tele-vid screen on the wall in front of them flashed into life, and Liz's heart missed a beat when she saw Harry standing aboard *Explorer*. On either side of him were indeed Kate and Joanne. Behind them were several other crewmembers, being closely watched by some pirate guards.

Along with some familiar pirate faces – Tarik and Dork – was McDuff, presumably of more use on his old ship than in the prison camp. He looked a little uncomfortable, and Liz wondered if that now their release was a serious possibility, he was realising just how short-sighted his treachery had been.

Liz noted Harry's expression of shock and anger, and from the gamut of emotions flashing in his eyes she realised that he could see her too.

'Hello, my dear Clarke,' said Valdez, his tone disturbingly calm and confident. 'We meet again. I presume you've been warned by my colleagues not to speak – just listen.' Harry nodded. 'Good. Well, as you can see I am just entertaining someone who, I know, is of great importance to you, while you and your two charming code-holders turn off the self-destruct mechanism of *Explorer*. I thought it best to keep her here with me,' he patted her nearest forearm, 'just to make sure you don't get any silly ideas. A little insurance policy, you might say.'

His hand moved slowly up her arm, to her shoulder, and then on and he lightly fingered the collar. 'Hartley has already experienced the ingenuity of this little toy,' he continued. 'But it gets better. You see, my dear

Clarke, this deceptively insignificant looking collar has been programmed to the same frequency as the self-destruct mechanism on *Explorer*. It will activate in ten minutes unless it receives the disarm code which you will shortly feed in. Once activated it will slowly but relentless contract, agonisingly choking the very life out of your precious second-in-command.

'So, if you have any misguided notions about being a hero, think again.' He cupped Liz's chin in a powerful grip to make sure Harry could clearly see the dread freezing her expression. 'You would undoubtedly be exterminated by my colleagues, and you would also be signing this lovely creature's death warrant. Can you imagine that, Clarke? Can you imagine being not only responsible for your death and that of the colleagues with you, but also for the death of this young lady, who means more to you than anything else?' He paused, letting the full impact of his words sink in. His confident smile never wavered.

'I can see from your expression that you can. You have less than nine minutes remaining before this ingenious collar commences and concludes its most regrettable duty.' His eyes flashed victoriously at the screen before he continued.

'If, however, you do as you're told, your period of captivity will soon be over. We shall let you go in another ship. The Federation has made a few token concessions for the release of you and your crew.'

Liz guessed that the Federation wouldn't have given

much ground. She surmised that the pirates would have already achieved good propaganda from their captives and now had little more need of them.

'Just to confirm to you that Hartley has been well looked after by us and is still in good shape,' Valdez was continuing, 'I will permit her to say a few words. My dear?' He turned to Liz and gestured towards the screen.

Liz realised it was her one and only chance.

'Valdez,' she said to her tormentor, instead of speaking to Harry, 'even if I respected you half as much – *half*, I say – as I do my captain, I still wouldn't give you the satisfaction of pleading for mercy. The captain and the others know what they must do.' She spoke defiantly with blazing eyes.

Valdez looked thoughtfully for a moment, and Liz's heart skipped a beat; had she made her cryptic message about altering the codes too obvious?

'Still brimming with misguided valour, eh?' Valdez said, unable to hide his evident respect for her. 'I love a spirit like yours... and I particularly love breaking a spirit like yours.' He fixed her with his icy stare, admiring her stoic beauty, and then turned back to the screen.

'Do as you have been instructed within the next eight minutes, Clarke, and we can then think about your release.' He pressed the remote and the image on the screen instantly shut down.

'You bastard,' Liz whispered venomously, but Valdez

213

merely laughed and stood up.

'Now, now,' he chuckled. 'Is that any way to speak to your host? I would have expected better manners from someone of your station, my dear.'

Before Liz could curse again he turned to Sulin. 'Keep an eye on her,' he ordered. 'I shall be back soon. I'm just going to monitor events on *Explorer*. You may amuse yourself for a few minutes, if you wish.'

Liz's stomach churned at the feel of that frightful collar around her throat again. She prayed that if the alternative codes were used to delay, rather than disarm, the self-destruct, they would not activate the murderous device. Then her thoughts were interrupted as Sulin moved closer, and Liz saw the lustful look in her eye as she gazed down upon her pinioned body.

'Now then, Hartley,' Sulin purred. 'You heard what my superior said. Shall we have ourselves a little fun?'

Liz closed her eyes against the continuing torment. The threat of something going wrong with Harry, and the collar starting its grim deed in only a few minutes, was compounded by being at the mercy of the lecherous woman. She felt fingers on her tunic, moving lightly, and then the top button popped open. The strain on the material caused it to spring a little further apart, exposing more of her cleavage to Sulin.

'How enchanting,' sighed the woman. Another button gave up the struggle, but the broad strap that highlighted the mouth-watering thrust of Liz's bosom hampered further progress. Undaunted, Sulin eased persistent

214

fingers inside the tunic and cupped one warm breast. 'Oh yes,' she cooed. 'Now that *does* feel nice.'

With eyes still closed, trying to dismiss what was happening to her, Liz heard movement, and then felt warm lips touch hers. 'Open your mouth,' Sulin whispered. 'Open…'

Liz reluctantly obeyed, and could do nothing but accept the tongue that probed inside. The kiss became more passionate as the intrusive fingers found her nipple and stroked it, causing her to groan a little, despite herself.

'Mmmm… you're *so* sexy,' Sulin enthused. 'I wish we had more time together. I'd soon help you forget Harry Clarke – or any other man, for that matter.' She lowered herself a little more and moulded her breasts against Liz's, grinding softly.

No matter how intense her loathing for anyone connected with the pirate empire, and despite the fact that she may only have minutes left before the collar activated, Liz couldn't suppress the shameful excitement the woman's touch and closeness was evoking. With her free hand Sulin gently stroked Liz's hair, and pulled her closer for another lingering kiss that made Liz's nipple stiffen between the knowing fingers.

At that moment the door opened and Valdez returned, smiling even more arrogantly than before.

'You'll be pleased to hear, my dear,' he said, watching with amusement as Sulin hastily broke away from the sensuous embrace, even though he'd given her permission to indulge herself, 'that Clarke has been a very sensible chap.' He immediately detected the erotic charge in the room, but continued anyway. '*Explorer* is now ours, and the collar will therefore remain impotent.' He chuckled. 'Never let it be said that I am not a man of my word.' He moved closer and reclaimed his place on the stool beside Liz.

'Now, my dear,' he said, taking his time to get comfortable, 'my wife tell's me you're more than a little receptive to attentions from one of your own gender. I think we have a little time to relax and celebrate, so why don't you two lovely creatures just carry on as you were?'

Chapter Twenty-Two

The pirates had put *Explorer's* crew into one of their old vessels, the *Colossus*, but Liz still had grave doubts as to the credibility of their word. It all seemed too easy, but they had no other realistic choice. Perhaps the pirate nation had decided they could squeeze no more concessions from the Federation, they possessed something of immense value and importance in *Explorer*, and the prisoner crew was now an unnecessary liability.

But it still seemed all too easy. She was sure the devious pirates would have planned something, that there would yet be a sting in the tail.

They were allowed to ease the *Colossus* out of its dock and begin the journey out of the Magellan system. Although, ominously, they saw *Explorer* fired up and ready to move, they had no choice but to keep going and move out.

And the serene grace of the old ship's gliding departure belied the frantic activity within her hull. Although the old freighter had been stripped of any transmitting device from which they could summon help, every minute that they continued on their way without signs of pursuit increased their odds of survival.

To the watching pirates the *Colossus* seemed to take

a long time to get properly on its way. They assumed it was the crew's unfamiliarity with the vessel. Eventually, however, they were away from the close proximity of the spaceport and gathering speed. Then Valdez and his key players boarded *Explorer* before it too nosed out of dock. Although their other vessels would now have difficulty in overhauling the freighter, they knew that the ex-Federation vessel would catch it within the hour.

On the bridge of the *Colossus* Harry and Liz watched *Explorer* tracking them, and gaining relentlessly. They looked at each other, saying nothing, but knowing that their plan would now be put to the ultimate test, and their lives and the lives of their crew depended on the outcome.

They had no weapons or means of defending themselves, and it was clear that they were soon to become target practice for the new owners of their ship.

Ever nearer it stalked, looking awesomely threatening both on the bridge monitors and through the bridge windows. Without taking her eyes from the predatory warship creeping up on them, Liz felt for and then held Harry's hand, and an awful silence fell over the bridge. There was a sudden cessation of any activity as everyone stopped still where they sat or stood, and many fearful eyes watched the monitors or looked with dread out of the windows. For a second Liz had some sympathy for the many pirates who must have experienced the awful feeling she now felt as they'd looked at the threatening spectre she now looked at. She tried to remember the number of 'kills' that had been credited to *Explorer*, but the figure, previously etched indelibly on her mind, now escaped her.

Then *Explorer's* weapon systems must have locked onto *Colossus* because, suddenly, they all flinched and squinted as a blinding flash of light filled the screens and windows.

The delayed action code *had* worked! Kate had managed to warn Joanne about halving the sequence numbers, and Harry, prevented from communicating with either of them by the pirate guards, had gambled on the meaning of Liz's veiled message.

There were no dry eyes as their faithful ship was vaporised amongst the other atoms in the fabric of space. Liz felt Harry's hand give hers a return squeeze, and then they all prepared for the long journey home in the unfamiliar vessel.

That evening Liz relaxed for the first time in what seemed a lifetime, in the privacy of her own cabin. It wasn't as big as hers had been on *Explorer*, but it was a palace compared to the pirate's hospitality.

She had downed a large glass of iced wine, briefly running over the astro calculations again in her mind, satisfying herself that they were on course for Earth and had sufficient speed to stay well clear of any pursuing pirate vessels. A broad smile lit up her face as she thought about the little parting gift she'd left for

Rolf, Koolin, and Stone. She checked the time, and realised it would have announced itself with devastating results shortly beforehand.

She answered a knock at the door with a groan; was it another problem with the unfamiliar equipment?

Harry stood in the corridor, grinning at her.

When the door was shut safely behind him the two gazed at each other in silence, their eyes saying everything. He moved, a little awkwardly like a bashful teenager wanting to hold a girl for the first time, and cocooned her in his strength.

At last Liz felt safe. They inched back together and, without breaking the comforting embrace, lay down on her bunk. They rocked gently together, and then Harry kissed Liz's forehead as she fell asleep in his arms.

Exciting titles available from Chimera

All **Chimera** titles are/will be available from your local bookshop or newsagent, or direct from our mail order department. Please send your order with a cheque or postal order (made payable to *Chimera Publishing Ltd*) to: **Chimera Publishing Ltd., PO Box 152, Waterlooville, Hants, PO8 9FS**. If you would prefer to pay by credit card, please call our **24 hour telephone/fax credit card hotline: +44 (0)23 92 783037**.

To order, send: Title, author, ISBN number and price for each book ordered, your full name and address, cheque or postal order payable to B.B.C.S. for the total amount, and allow the following for postage and packing:
UK and BFPO: £1.00 for the first book, and 50p for each additional book to a maximum of £3.50.
Overseas and Eire: £2.00 for the first book, £1.00 for the second and 50p for each additional book.

*Titles £5.99 (US$9.95). All others £4.99 (US$7.95)

For details about the **Chimera Readers' Club** or for a copy of our free catalogue please write to:

Chimera Publishing Ltd
Readers' Services
PO Box 152
Waterlooville
Hants
PO8 9FS

Or visit our WebShop at:
www.chimerabooks.co.uk